"I Won't Sleep With You, Jared."

"And I told you, Dana, that I won't push you into doing anything you aren't ready for."

She lifted a confused brow. "And what do you think you're doing now?"

He shrugged. "Attempting to destroy your theory that sex is overrated. But I don't have to sleep with you to do that."

"You don't?"

"No."

Dana swallowed. She believed him. Now she understood why he was one of the most successful attorneys in Atlanta. "You're smooth," she said. He was using every weapon at his disposal to break down her defenses. There was the huskiness of his voice, the look of heated desire in his eyes and his aroused body. Even his stance was provocatively sexy.

"I'm also thorough."

Dear Reader,

This May, Silhouette Desire's sensational lineup starts with Nalini Singh's *Awaken the Senses.* This DYNASTIES: THE ASHTONS title is a tale of sexual awakening starring one seductive Frenchman. (Can you say ooh-la-la?) Also for your enjoyment this month is the launch of Maureen Child's trilogy. The THREE-WAY WAGER series focuses on the Reilly brothers, triplets who bet each other they can stay celibate for ninety days. But wait until brother number one is reunited with *The Tempting Mrs. Reilly.*

Susan Crosby's BEHIND CLOSED DOORS series continues with *Heart of the Raven,* a gothic-toned story of a man whose self-imposed seclusion has cut him off from love…until a sultry woman, and a beautiful baby, open up his heart. Brenda Jackson is back this month with a new Westmoreland story, in *Jared's Counterfeit Fiancée,* the tale of a fake engagement that leads to real passion. Don't miss Cathleen Galitz's *Only Skin Deep,* a delightful transformation story in which a shy girl finally falls into bed with the man she's always dreamed about. And rounding out the month is *Bedroom Secrets* by Michelle Celmer, featuring a hero to die for.

Thanks for choosing Silhouette Desire, where we strive to bring you the best in smart, sensual romances. And in the months to come look for a new installment of our TEXAS CATTLEMAN'S CLUB continuity and a brand-new TANNERS OF TEXAS title from the incomparable Peggy Moreland.

Happy reading!

Melissa Jeglinski

Melissa Jeglinski
Senior Editor
Silhouette Books

Please address questions and book requests to:
Silhouette Reader Service
U.S.: 3010 Walden Ave., P.O. Box 1325, Buffalo, NY 14269
Canadian: P.O. Box 609, Fort Erie, Ont. L2A 5X3

JARED'S
COUNTERFEIT
FIANCÉE

BRENDA JACKSON

Silhouette® Desire

Published by Silhouette Books

America's Publisher of Contemporary Romance

SILHOUETTE BOOKS

ISBN 0-373-76654-8

JARED'S COUNTERFEIT FIANCÉE

This edition published by arrangement with Harlequin Books S.A.

® and TM are trademarks of Harlequin Books S.A., used under license. Trademarks indicated with ® are registered in the United States Patent and Trademark Office, the Canadian Trade Marks Office and in other countries.

Visit Silhouette Books at www.eHarlequin.com

Printed in U.S.A.

Books by Brenda Jackson

Silhouette Desire

*Westmoreland family titles

BRENDA JACKSON

is a die "heart" romantic who married her childhood sweetheart and still proudly wears the "going steady" ring he gave her when she was fifteen. Because she's always believed in the power of love, Brenda's stories always have happy endings. In her real-life love story, Brenda and her husband of thirty-three years live in Jacksonville, Florida, and have two sons.

A USA TODAY bestselling author, Brenda divides her time between family, writing and working in management at a major insurance company. You may write Brenda at P.O. Box 28267, Jacksonville, Florida 32226, by e-mail at WriterBJackson@aol.com or visit her Web site at www.brendajackson.net.

To my husband Gerald Jackson, Sr., with all my love.
To my family and friends for their continued support.
To Dr. Angela Martin, GYN. Thanks for all your
invaluable information.

An intelligent man is always open to new ideas.
In fact he looks for them.
—*Proverbs* 18:15

Prologue

Jared Westmoreland glanced up from the legal document he'd been reading when he heard a commotion outside of his office door.

He heard his secretary say, "Wait a minute, miss. You just can't barge into Mr. Westmoreland's office unannounced," moments before his door flew open and a gorgeous but angry woman stormed in.

Jared's heart rate quickened and his pulse accelerated. He forced back the blatant desire that rushed through him as he walked from behind his desk. The woman was absolutely stunning. Even her apparent anger didn't detract from her beauty. In one smooth glance, he took in a mass of dark brown curls that framed her face and the smooth, creamy texture of her skin—the color of rich mahogany. Then there were her beautiful dark brown eyes with perfectly arched brows, a delectable pair of lips and rounded cheeks with dimples that not even her anger could hide. A sleek, curvy body in a pair of slacks and a tailored blouse completed the vision of beauty.

"Mr. Westmoreland, I tried to stop her but she—"

"That's all right, Jeannie," Jared said to his secretary, who had raced in behind the woman.

"Do you want me to call security?"

"No, I don't think that will be necessary."

Jeannie Tillman, who'd worked for him for over five years, didn't look too convinced. "Are you sure?"

He stared at the seething woman who was standing with both hands on her hips, glaring at him. "Yes, I'm sure." Jeannie gave him a hesitant nod and turned to leave, closing the door behind her.

Jared turned his full attention to his beautiful intruder. He was fairly certain that she was not a client since he didn't forget a beautiful face. In fact, he was sure he'd never met her before.

Dana Rollins met Jared's stare and tried to keep her intense reaction to him from showing. She had heard about Jared Westmoreland, Atlanta's hotshot, millionaire attorney. Now she was seeing him for herself and it seemed that all she'd heard was true. He was definitely the stuff dreams were made of. A sharp dresser, all the way down to his expensive-looking leather shoes, he was tall, with a body that was well built. Solid as a rock. He had coffee-colored skin, dark brown eyes, a solid jaw, straight nose and close-cut black hair. They were handsome features on a sensual face; the kind that would definitely make her do a double take. But she couldn't dwell on how sexy he looked. She was here for business and nothing more.

"I'm sure there's a reason why you barged into my office, Miss…"

"Rollins," she supplied sharply. His words reminded her of what that business was. "And yes, there is a reason. This!" she said, pulling an envelope out of her purse. "I received this certified letter from you less than an hour ago demanding that I return my engagement ring to Luther. I tried calling him but was told he's out of town so I immediately came here to get an explanation."

Jared took the letter from her and looked at it. The assessment didn't take long. He glanced back at her. "I gather you have a problem with returning the ring, Miss Rollins?" he asked.

"Of course I do. Luther decided he wasn't ready to give up his single status and called off our wedding a week before it was to take place. Besides the embarrassment and humiliation of everything—explaining things to my friends and returning shower gifts—I was left with all the wedding expenses. And to pour salt on the wound, I received that letter from your firm."

Jared inhaled deeply. Evidently she hadn't yet realized that Luther Cord had done her a favor. "Miss Rollins, I suggest you consult your own attorney to verify what I'm telling you, but my client has every right to ask for the engagement ring back. An engagement ring represents a conditional gift. The proposition is that the condition is marriage and not a willingness to marry. Thus if the engagement is broken, for whatever reason, the expectation is that the ring is returned, just as you returned the wedding presents and shower gifts," he said.

He watched as she crossed her arms over her chest and the angry frown on her lips deepened and turned rebellious. "I refuse to give it back. It's the principle of the thing."

Jared shook his head thinking that principle had nothing to do with it. The law was the law. "Unfortunately, Miss Rollins, you're faced with a losing battle and a very costly one. Do you want to add a bunch of legal fees to everything else right now?"

He knew the mention of finances would help make her think straight. And knowing he had her thinking in the right direction, he pressed forward. "I know what you're going through must be painful, but my advice to you is to try and put this episode behind you and move on. You're a beautiful woman, and I believe there's a man out there who's truly worthy of you. Evidently Luther Cord isn't. Perhaps you should count your blessings."

Jared knew his words weren't what she wanted to hear but he wanted to be as honest with her as he could. There was only so much he could say, considering the fact that Luther Cord was his client. In fact, he had said too much already. But for some reason he wanted to help end her heartache as soon as possible.

Moments passed and Dana didn't say anything, but he could tell she was thinking about what he'd said. Then he watched as she pulled a small white box from her purse and handed it to him.

He met her gaze when she said softly, "I appreciate your advice and although it's a bitter pill to swallow, I'll return the ring."

He flipped it open and saw the dazzling diamond solitaire before placing the small box on his desk. "You're doing the right thing, Miss Rollins."

She nodded and extended her hand to him. "The last thing I need is to get into more debt. Luther isn't worth it."

He accepted her hand, liking the way it fit neatly into his. "I hope things work out for you," he said with complete sincerity.

Dana gazed intently into his eyes and smiled appreciatively. Although she hadn't wanted to hear what he'd said, she couldn't help but be grateful for his honesty. In her experience, compassion and kindness were two emotions attorneys seldom possessed. "Somehow they will. I know I interrupted your work by barging in here the way I did and I apologize," she said.

"You didn't interrupt anything," Jared said smoothly. "And as for my advice, consider it a favor."

The smile that touched her lips widened. "Thanks. Maybe I'll be able to return the favor some day. I owe you one."

As he released her hand and watched her turn and walk out of his office, Jared thought to himself that Dana Rollins was as sensual as a woman could get.

One

A month later

Jared Westmoreland was having one hell of a morning.

It began with the message his mother had left on his answering machine last night, reminding him that his father's and his uncle's birthdays fell on Easter Sunday this year and requesting that he set an example for his five brothers by bringing a date to the huge dinner party she and his aunt Evelyn had planned.

His cousin Storm's recent wedding had made his mother, Sarah, take stock and realize that her six sons had yet to show serious interest in any woman. And of course, since he was the eldest, she felt he should be the first and had every intention of prodding him in the right direction. It didn't matter that he and his brothers were successful and enjoyed being single. She felt that the only way any of them could truly be happy was to find that special woman and tie the knot. The only one who wasn't experiencing the heat was his brother Spencer, whose fiancée Lynette, had died in a drowning accident three years ago.

Jared rose from his chair and walked over to the window. To add to the annoyance of his mother's call, he had arrived at work an hour later than usual because of traffic. And as if things couldn't get any worse, he had just received a phone call from entertainer Sylvester Brewster, who wanted to file for a divorce—from wife number three. Sylvester was good for business, but it was hard to watch him involve himself in relationships that didn't last.

When Jared heard the buzzer sounding on his desk, he turned around and sighed heavily, wondering if the morning could get any worse. Crossing the room he picked up the phone. "Yes, Jeannie?"

"Mr. Westmoreland, your mother is on the line."

Jared shook his head. Yes, his morning could get worse. It just did. "Go ahead and put her through."

A few moments later after hearing the connection, he said. "Hi, Mom."

"Did you get my message, Jared?"

Jared raised his gaze to the ceiling before saying. "Yes, I got it."

"Good. Then I'll be setting an extra plate out for dinner next Sunday."

Jared wanted to tell her in a nice, respectable way that if she set out the plate there was a strong chance it would sit there empty. But before he could get the words out, his mother quickly added, "Remember, you're the oldest and I expect you to set an example. Besides, you're not getting any younger."

She made it seem as if he was fifty-seven instead of thirty-seven. Besides, his mother knew how he felt about the institution of marriage. He was a divorce attorney for heaven's sake. He ended marriages, not put them together. He'd handled enough divorce cases to know that marriage wasn't all it was cracked up to be. People got married and then a lot of them eventually got divorced. It was a vicious cycle; one that made him money, but sickened him at the same time. Although there were long-lasting marriages in the Westmoreland family, he considered them exceptions and not the norm. It would be just his luck to have the first failed marriage in the family and he had no intention of becoming a statistic.

"Jared, are you listening?"

He sighed. When she used that tone, he had no other choice but to listen. "Yes, but has it occurred to you that Durango, Ian, Spencer, Quade, Reggie and I like being single?" he asked respectfully.

"And has it ever occurred to any of you that your father and I aren't getting any younger and we'd love to have grandchildren while we're still of sound mind to enjoy them?"

Jared shook his head. First, she was trying to shove marriage down their throats and now she was hinting at grandchildren. But he was smart enough to know that the last thing he needed was to butt heads with caring, stubborn Sarah Westmoreland. He would rather face an uncompromising judge in the courtroom than oppose his mother. It was an uphill battle that he just didn't have the energy for right now.

"I'll see what I can do," he finally said.

"Thanks, Son. That's all I ask."

"Really, Dana, I wish you would think about going with us."

Dana Rollins glanced up at Cybil Franklin, who stood in the middle of her office with a determined frown on her face. Cybil was Dana's best friend from high school and the primary reason she had relocated from Tennessee to Atlanta three years ago to take a position at Kessler Industries as a landscape architect.

"Thanks, Cybil, but I'm sure you've heard the saying that three's a crowd. I don't think going with you and Ben to North Carolina this weekend is a good idea."

Cybil rolled her eyes. "It's just a camping trip to the mountains. I feel awful knowing you'll be spending Easter alone."

Leaning back in the chair behind her desk, Dana smiled easily. "Hey, I'm a twenty-seven-year-old woman who can take care of herself. I'll be fine and I have no problem spending Easter alone." *It will be just like every other year since Mom and Dad died.*

None of the holidays were the same anymore since her parents had been killed in a car accident on their way to her college graduation five years earlier. Since she had no other family, their deaths had left her truly alone. She'd thought all that had changed when she met Luther. They began dating in early spring and after six months, he had asked her to marry him.

"It's times like these when I'm tempted to find

Luther Cord and kill him," Cybil said angrily. "When I think of what he did to you, I get so mad."

Dana smiled softly, no longer able to muster up anger when she thought about Luther. He had paid her an unexpected visit last week to tell her that he was moving to California. He told her that his decision not to marry had nothing to do with her, that he'd come to terms with his sexual preference, and that in his own way he loved her, but not in the way a husband is supposed to love his wife. At first she had been shocked, but then she'd acknowledged that the signs had all been there. She couldn't, or hadn't wanted to see them. Dana hadn't told anyone about Luther's confession, not even Cybil.

Dana turned her attention back to her friend. "I told you that I'd be fine. It won't be the first or the last holiday that I spend alone."

"I know but I wish that—"

"Cybil, let it go. You need to get out of here if you're meeting Ben for lunch," she said, trying to propel her out the door.

"Okay, but call me soon?"

As soon as Cybil left, Dana released a huge sigh.

Since her breakup with Luther, Dana put all of her time and energy into her job. Work wasn't a substitute for having a family and a personal life, but it did take her mind off her loneliness.

She glanced at the calendar on her desk. It was hard to believe next week was Easter already. Her parents would make every holiday special and even while in college she enjoyed going home during spring break to spend Easter with them. She remembered their last

Easter together. They had gone to sunrise church service and later they had feasted on the delicious dinner her mother had prepared, not knowing it would be the last holiday meal they would share together.

She sighed deeply, not wanting to relinquish the memories just yet but knowing that she had to. Somehow she would get through another holiday without her parents. She had no other choice.

"What would you like to order, sir?"

Jared studied the huge menu posted on the wall behind the counter and made his decision. "Umm, give me a ham and cheese all the way on whole wheat, an order of French fries and a glass of sweetened tea."

"All right. Your order will be ready in a minute."

Jared nodded then glanced around. Usually he met clients for lunch at restaurants that served the finest cuisine; and at other times he would order in and eat lunch at his office. But he had decided to take advantage of how beautiful a day it was and walk the block from his office to the deli.

The place was crowded and he hoped that he would be able to find a seat by the time his lunch was ready. He was even willing to share a table or booth with someone if the person didn't have a problem with it.

As his eyes scanned the crowded restaurant, he tried to find someone sitting alone. Abruptly his gaze stopped on a familiar-looking woman at a booth, who was reading a book while leisurely munching on a French fry. A memory suddenly flared in his mind, jump-started his senses and instantly stirred heat within him.

Dana Rollins.

It had been a month since she had stormed into his office, but he vividly recalled the impact she'd made on his male senses when she'd barged in that day. He felt blood race through his veins, reminding him that he'd been so busy at work, he hadn't been with a woman in over eight months.

He was accustomed to beautiful, gorgeous women, but there was something intrinsically special about Dana Rollins. He hadn't been this attracted to a woman since heaven knows when. Now it seemed he was making up for lost time.

"Sir, your order is ready."

Jared turned and took the tray loaded with his food from the man behind the counter. "Thanks." He then glanced back over at Dana Rollins and after making a quick decision, he crossed the room to where she sat.

She was so absorbed in her book that she didn't notice him standing next to her. She was leaning forward with both her elbows on the table while holding the book in front of her, so that the neckline of her blouse gapped open enough for him to get a generous glimpse of her cleavage. He liked what he saw—firm, full breasts.

Knowing he couldn't stand there and continue to ogle her, he cleared his throat. "Miss Rollins?"

She quickly glanced up and recognized him. He watched her shimmering bronze lips tilt into a smile guaranteed to turn him on. "Mr. Westmoreland, it's good to see you again."

Her dimpled smile made him acutely aware of just how beautiful she was. "It's good seeing you again, too. It's rather crowded in here and I saw you sitting alone and wondered if perhaps I could join you?"

Her smile widened into a grin. "Yes, of course," she said, placing her book down on the table, making sure not to lose her spot.

"Thanks," he said, sliding into the seat across from her in the booth. "How have you been?"

Her lashes fluttered downward before sweeping up with her gaze to meet his. "I've been fine and have done what you suggested and moved on."

Jared nodded. "I'm glad to hear it, Miss Rollins."

Her smile widened. "Please call me Dana."

He chuckled. "Only if you call me Jared."

After saying grace, he took a sip of his drink then proceeded to put ketchup on his fries. He glanced her way and smiled. "So what are you reading?"

She took a sip of her drink then picked up the book and held it up. "A book of poems by Maya Angelou. She's a wonderful poet and I love reading her work. It can be so uplifting."

He nodded. He had read several of her poems himself. Dana met his gaze. "Do you read a lot, Jared?"

He shrugged broad shoulders under an expensive suit. "The only pleasure reading I have time for these days is my cousin's novels. He writes under the pen name Rock Mason."

Her eyes lit up and showed her surprise. "You're related to Rock Mason?"

Jared laughed. "Yes. His real name is Stone Westmoreland."

Dana smiled. "Wow. I've read all of his books. He's a gifted writer."

Jared chuckled. "I'll make sure I tell him you said that when I see him again. He and his wife, Madison, are in Texas visiting cousins we have there, but they'll be back for our fathers' birthdays next weekend."

"Your fathers' birthdays?"

He smiled. "Our fathers are fraternal twins and they turn sixty this year. Since their birthdays fall on Easter Sunday, our mothers are hosting one huge celebration."

"Sounds like all of you will have a wonderful time."

He chuckled. "We usually do when we all get together. The Westmoreland family is big. What about you? Are you from a large family?"

He watched sadness appear in her eyes. "I don't have any family. I was an only child and my parents were killed five years ago in an auto accident en route to my college graduation."

"I'm sorry."

She met his gaze and saw the sincerity of his words. "Thank you. It was hard for me, but I got through it. Since my parents didn't have any siblings, and their parents are deceased, I don't have a family."

He watched as she caught her lower lip between her teeth as if to keep it from trembling with the remembered pain. "What are your plans for Easter Sunday?" he couldn't help but ask.

"I don't have any. I'll go to a sunrise service at church and will probably spend the rest of the day at home relaxing and reading."

He lifted an eyebrow. "What about dinner?"

She shrugged. "I'll pull out a microwave dinner and enjoy the day that way."

Jared tried shifting his attention back to his food but couldn't fully concentrate on what he was eating. Because of his large family, he had grown up loving the holidays and even looked forward to them, although lately his mother's interfering had tempered his anticipation.

An idea suddenly popped into Jared's head. His mother was expecting him to bring someone to dinner so why not Dana? When his mother and his aunt Evelyn got together, the two women cooked up a storm. That had to be better than a microwave dinner. "How would you like to join me for Easter dinner at my parents' home?" He could tell that his invitation surprised her.

"You're inviting me to dinner at your parents' place?"

"Yes."

She shook her head, as if still not understanding. "But, why? We barely know each other."

Jared knew he had to level with her. "It just so happens that you can help me out of a jam."

Dana lifted a brow. "What kind of jam?"

"My mother is obsessed. Lately, a number of my cousins have gotten married and since none of her six sons are rushing to follow suit, she's taken it upon herself to prod us along. I'm the oldest so I'm feeling the heat more than the others. She expects me to set an example by bringing someone to dinner. And since I recall you owe me a favor, I figured now's the time to collect."

Dana blinked and then she released a deep sigh. Jared could tell she had forgotten about her promise. "But I'm sure there're plenty of women you've dated who would love going to dinner with you at your parents' home," she implored.

Jared nodded as he continued to smile. "Yes, but if I take any of them they might get the wrong impression and think that I'm actually interested in a serious relationship. Besides, my mother and aunt are good cooks. All you'll have to do is show up with me, endure the likes of my family and join in with the birthday festivities. I understand it's a lot to ask, but I'd really appreciate it if you'd come. It will definitely get Mom off my back."

Jared watched as she nervously gnawed her bottom lip. He had presented the situation just as it was.

Dana met his gaze. She had felt that pull between them, that physical attraction, so to consider being in Jared's company for any reason wasn't a good idea. But, she did owe him a favor and she'd always been taught to keep her word. "And it's just this one time?"

"Yes, just this one time," he assured her. "But to pull this off, we'll need a convincing story. I think it would be a good idea if I called you one day this week to discuss answers to the questions I have a feeling my family will ask."

Dana frowned. "What kind of questions?"

Jared grinned. "Oh, the usual, like how long have we known each other? When and how we met? How serious are things between us? And there's a strong chance my mother might get downright personal and want to know if you've moved in with me yet, whether you're capable of producing babies and if so, how many you're willing to have."

Dana blinked, then laughed out loud. Jared thought it was a beautiful sound; and in all honesty, the deep rumble in her throat was a blatant turn-on.

"You aren't serious, are you?" she asked, bringing her laughter under control.

He chuckled. "Unfortunately, I am. Just wait until you meet my mother for yourself. Marrying off one of her sons seems to be her number-one priority."

Dana raised an arched brow. "And marriage is something you have an aversion to?"

"Yes. I handle enough divorce cases to know that most marriages don't last."

He watched as she sat back in her chair with a thoughtful expression on her face. "So will you be my date that day?"

Dana considered Jared's invitation. After a few moments she nodded her agreement.

Jared smiled, pleased with the turn of events. "Thanks, Dana. I appreciate you helping me out of this jam. You don't know how much it means to be able to get my mother off my back."

Two

Dana glanced down at her watch. Jared was coming to pick her up at any moment and she was a nervous wreck.

They had talked on the phone earlier in the week to get prepared for his family's inquisition. Just hearing his voice had sent sensuous chills all through her body and reminded her that she was definitely a woman, something she had forgotten since her breakup with Luther.

That reminder came with a mixture of empowerment and restraint. The last thing she needed was to test emotional waters that were best left uncharted. All she had to do was remember what had happened with Luther to know that, woman or not, the last thing she wanted was to become vulnerable to any man again.

Dana almost jumped when she heard the sound of her doorbell. She inhaled deeply and reminded herself that she probably wouldn't see Jared again after today so there was no reason for her to come unglued. She released a sigh of relief and opened the door.

Jared gazed at Dana and quickly pulled in a deep breath. If he thought that she was gorgeous before, today she had surpassed his memories. He'd always had a healthy sex drive, but seeing her standing in the doorway with all that glorious hair spread over her shoulders and wearing a pair of jeans that hugged her curvy figure and a pretty knit top, had him wondering how he would get through the day.

"Hi, Jared, please come in."

"Thanks. You look nice."

She smiled and stepped back as he entered and closed the door behind him. "Thank you. I just need to grab my purse," she said, walking off toward a room he assumed was her bedroom.

He was glad for the extra time to pull himself together. The woman was sexy and feminine all rolled into one.

Trying to distract himself, he glanced around her living room. It was nicely decorated in bright colors and with upscale furnishings. He felt something rubbing against his leg and looked down and smiled. "Hey, where did you come from?" he asked, leaning down and picking up a beautiful black cat.

"I'm ready now," Dana said, reentering the room. She smiled when she saw him holding her cat. "I see you've met Tom."

Jared chuckled. "Oh, that's his name?"

"Yes. I've had him for a couple of years, since he was a kitten. Now he's spoiled rotten but great company."

"He's a handsome fellow," Jared said as he continued to pet the animal.

"Shh, don't say that too loud. He's conceited enough already," Dana whispered.

Jared smiled as he placed Tom back on the floor. When he straightened back to his full height he met Dana's gaze. Desire shot all the way through him and with an effort he swallowed. "Ready?" he asked.

"Yes, I'm ready."

"Welcome to our home, Dana. I'm so glad that Jared brought you."

Dana suddenly found herself swept into strong arms as a woman who she figured to be Jared's mother gave her a gigantic hug. She had expected a nice welcome but certainly not this outpouring of affection.

"Thanks for having me," Dana said once the woman released her. She glanced up at Jared. Their gazes met and held. His expression was unreadable and she couldn't help wondering what he was thinking.

Dana noticed a sudden thickness in her throat when she remembered how she'd felt when Jared had arrived at her place, exactly at noon. The only thing she could think was that even dressed in jeans and a pullover shirt he looked polished, suave, debonair and sensual.

"You two can give each other that dreamy-eyed look later," Sarah Westmoreland said, beaming. "Come on in, everyone is anxious to meet Dana."

Jared shook his head, catching himself and regaining his concentration. The last thing he wanted was for his mother to get any ideas that Dana was more than just a dinner date. "I take it that we're the last to arrive," he said, placing his hand at the small of Dana's back while his mother led them through the foyer.

"Quade isn't here but he called to say that he's on his way."

Jared nodded. His brother Quade was involved in security activities for the Secret Service and often missed family gatherings because of it. But it wasn't from lack of trying to be present. Like all Westmorelands, Quade enjoyed family get-togethers.

Jared could hear voices coming from the living room and took another look at Dana. He had intended it to be a quick look but even in the daylight, the soft glow from the crystal chandelier overhead seemed to enhance her beauty. There was something about the shape of her mouth—he wondered how it would feel under his when he…

"My goodness, Jared, will you stop staring at Dana like that!" his mother scolded in a chuckling voice.

Damn. He hadn't realized he'd been staring again. He kept forgetting just how observant his mother was; her eyes missed nothing. His mother was smiling and for the first time he wondered if perhaps he had made a mistake in inviting Dana. If his mother noticed his attention to her, he could just imagine what the other family members would think. That meant he had to keep his cool and not appear so taken with her.

"It's about time you got here."

Jared's head jerked around and he frowned. His brother Durango, the man who thought all women were made for his pleasure unless they had another man's stamp on them, was talking to Jared, but looking at Dana.

"Durango," Jared acknowledged when his brother came to join them.

Durango nodded but his gaze went straight back to Dana. "And who is this beautiful creature?" he asked smoothly, as a smile touched both corners of his mouth.

"This is Jared's girl. And she's off-limits to you, so behave," Sarah Westmoreland spoke up.

Jared's girl. Jared rubbed the back of his neck, feeling the heat already.

"Are you sure that you don't want any more birthday cake, Dana?"

Dana smiled at Sarah. "Thanks for asking but I don't think I can eat a single thing more. All the food was wonderful, Mrs. Westmoreland."

Dana was completely overwhelmed when Jared had escorted her into the living room and introduced her to his family. The house had been decorated with birthday streamers and balloons from corner to corner. It didn't take long to see that the Westmorelands weren't just a clan but a whole whopping village. The love and warmth between them was easy to see and feel.

There were Jared's male cousins, Dare, Thorn, Stone, Chase, Storm, Clint and Cole. They all favored each other and it was easy to tell they were kin. There were few women in the Westmoreland family: Jared's cousin Delaney who was married to a Middle East sheikh, a tall, dark, handsome man; his cousin Casey who lived in Texas and was sister to Clint and Cole, as well as Shelly, Tara, Madison and Jayla, the wives of Dare, Thorn, Stone and Storm. She also met Jared's uncle Corey and his wife, Abby.

She had never seen so many relatives gathered in one place before, and for a moment a part of her had felt a tinge of jealousy that some people had such a huge family while others had none. But that bout of jealousy soon dissolved when she saw just how friendly and down-to-earth everyone was. At first they had been curious because Jared had never brought a woman to any family function before, but eventually they began to treat her like one of the family, without hesitation, but with a few questions that she felt she effectively answered to satisfy their curiosity. When Jared's brother Quade arrived, all of the attention had momentarily shifted off her, but now it was back on her again.

Jayla was pregnant with twins and the women invited Dana to join them on a shopping trip they had planned for next weekend to help select items for the babies' nursery. Since Dana knew Jared intended for this to be the last time she socialized with his family, she declined, coming up with an excuse about all the errands she had to do Saturday morning, but had thanked them for the invitation.

She glanced over to where Jared stood talking to his brothers and cousins and her heart thumped an unsteady beat just watching him. As if he felt her looking at him, he cocked his head in her direction and their gazes connected. Goose bumps skittered along her arms and she expelled a long, silent breath before breaking eye contact with him.

Needing to distract herself, she glanced out of the window. Jared's parents' home sat on three acres of land and the huge, two-story, Southern style structure was simply stunning. A huge window provided a view of a lake. It was late afternoon and getting dark, which was a stark indication that Easter was almost over.

"I need to talk to you privately for a moment," Jared whispered softly in her ear.

She sucked in a sharp breath. She hadn't heard him approach and the warmth of his breath touched her neck and the faint spicy aroma of his aftershave made her skin tingle.

She wondered what he had to talk to her about and knew his family wondered, as well, when he took her hand and guided her into the kitchen, closing the door behind them.

He leaned against the kitchen counter and for a moment they stared at each other, not saying anything. Then he cleared his throat. "I should have given you this earlier at your apartment when I picked you up but I forgot." Jared knew he could have waited until he returned her home, but for some reason he wanted to get her alone, even if only for a few minutes. "Luther Cord sent a special delivery to me on Friday with instructions that I give you this. After arriving in California he evidently had a change of heart and decided he wanted you to keep it."

Dana raised a curious brow as she watched Jared reach into his pocket to pull out a small white box. She immediately knew what it was. "My engagement ring?" she asked startled.

Jared saw the surprised, but pleased look on her face and couldn't help but smile. "Yes, it's for you," he said handing the small box to her.

"I knew it! I just knew she was the one!"

Jared jerked his head around when his mother burst through the kitchen door. Her face was all aglow.

"I happened to be passing by the door and heard the words engagement ring. Oh, Jared, you have made me so proud and happy," his mother exclaimed between bouts of laughter and tears of joy. She then hugged Dana. "Welcome to the family."

Jared's head began spinning when it became crystal clear what his mother had assumed. He was just about to open his mouth to set her straight when the kitchen door flew open again and his entire family poured in.

"What's going on?" Jared's father asked when he saw his wife in tears.

Again Jared opened his mouth to speak but his mother's voice drowned out any words he was about to say. "Jared and Dana. They just got engaged! He gave her a ring! Oh, I am so happy. I can't believe that one of my sons is finally settling down and getting married."

Jared and Dana suddenly became swamped with words of congratulation and well wishing. He glanced over at Dana and saw she was as shocked with the way things were escalating as he was. He reached over and gently squeezed her hand, hoping that he was assuring her that he would straighten things out. He knew that he should do so now but couldn't recall the last time he'd seen his mother this happy.

Sarah Westmoreland began crying again. "You have really made me happy today, Jared. Who would have thought that of all my sons you would have a change of heart about marriage? But I could feel the love flowing between the two of you when I opened the door and saw you standing there together."

Dana glanced over at Jared. She read the message in his eyes that clearly said: *Trust me, I'll get us out of this mess, but for now, please let my mother have her moment of happiness.* She gave him a silent nod to let him know she understood what he was asking. She inhaled deeply. Of all the misunderstandings she'd heard of, this one was definitely a doozy.

"Dana and I are leaving," Jared said, taking Dana's hand and leading her out of the kitchen.

"But—but we haven't celebrated your good news," his mother called out when he headed for the door.

He turned to look at his relatives, wanting to tell them that they wouldn't be celebrating it, either. They had followed the couple to the door and were crowded around them. He frowned at the "glad it's you and not me" look on the faces of the other single Westmoreland men. "I'll see everyone tomorrow," he told his family.

Then without saying another word and holding Dana's hand firmly in his, he walked out of his parents' house, closing the door behind him.

"I'm sorry about what happened back there," Jared said. Talk about the wrong information getting blown out of proportion. "I just couldn't tell my mother the truth. She was so happy."

Dana nodded. "I understand."

Jared lifted his head and gazed over at Dana, met her gaze and something about the way she was looking back at him told him that she really did understand. "Thank you."

She smiled. "You don't have to thank me. This was a special day for your family. I saw how happy your mother was when she'd thought we'd gotten engaged."

Jared nodded, grateful for her understanding. "I'll

talk to her tomorrow and straighten things out," he said quietly.

"All right."

Satisfied, Jared put his car in gear and backed out of his parents' driveway. At the first traffic light they came to, he glanced over and noticed the engagement ring was on Dana's finger. He frowned, remembering his mother's insistence that she put it on. For some reason he didn't like seeing her wearing Luther Cord's ring. "Now that you have the ring back what are you going to do with it?" he asked, trying to keep his voice neutral.

Dana glanced over at him before looking down at the ring. "What I had planned to do all along. Hock it and use the money to pay off the remaining wedding expenses. I'm surprised Luther returned it to me."

Jared wasn't surprised. During the last conversation he'd had with Cord, he had suggested that he do the decent thing and relieve some of the financial burden breaking the engagement had placed on Dana. He had strongly recommended that although he wasn't legally obligated to do so, he should consider letting her keep the ring. Evidently the man had taken his advice.

When the traffic light changed, Jared glanced over at Dana. Her eyes were closed and her head was back against the headrest. He couldn't stop the smile that touched his lips. No doubt this had been a tiring day for her. He was used to his huge family, but a stranger might be overwhelmed.

"Considering everything, do you regret going to my parents' home for dinner?" he couldn't help but ask.

Although she didn't open her eyes, a smile touched

her lips. "No, I had a wonderful time, Jared. Being around your family and seeing your closeness, brought back so many memories of how close I was to my parents and how they used to make every holiday so special for me." She opened her eyes, tilted her head to him and smiled. "I really appreciate you sharing your friendly, loving pack with me today."

The warm look Dana gave him sent heated sensations down Jared's spine. She might have enjoyed spending time with his family, but he could admit that he had actually enjoyed spending the day with her, as well. She was a charming person to be around and, unlike a lot of his other dates, Dana had not demanded his complete attention, by clinging to him or refusing to let him out of her sight.

He had watched how easily she had blended in with his family and how quickly she had won them over. He could see why his mother thought he had fallen for her.

Jared's hand tightened on the steering wheel. Thinking he was falling for her was one thing, but actually believing that he was engaged to her was another. How could his mother assume such a thing? She knew how he felt about marriage. Did she actually believe one woman could make him change his whole thought process on something he felt so strongly about?

Moments later he pulled into Dana's driveway and brought the car to a stop. He glanced over at her and saw that she had fallen asleep. He hated waking her but knew that he had to. So as not to startle her, he leaned over and softly whispered, "Dana, you're home."

He watched as her eyes slowly opened, then of its

own accord his gaze latched on to her lips, full, luscious, tempting. He would give anything to know how they tasted.

"I think I'd better walk you to the door," he said, fighting the urge to pull her into his arms and kiss her.

He watched as she took a deep breath and nodded. "All right."

Opening the door he got out of the car and walked around to open the door for her; then together they walked to her door. She turned to face him. "Thanks again, Jared, for such a beautiful day. It was special."

He nodded. He wanted to say that she was special, too, but knew that he couldn't. This was their only time together and he had to accept that. "Thanks for being my date. I'll talk to my mother tomorrow."

"Okay."

He watched as she put her key in the door and moments later she turned to him. She hesitated for a moment, then asked, "Would you like to come in for a drink?"

He suddenly decided that he wanted to go in, but not for the drink she was offering. He wanted to do something he'd been thinking of all day. "Yes, I'd like that."

He followed her inside, but when she headed toward the kitchen he placed his hand on her arm. "I can't think of a better way for this day to end than this," he said softly, before leaning down and gently capturing her mouth with his, needing to taste her as much as he needed to breathe.

Shivers of profound pleasure shot through every part of Dana's body the moment their lips touched and her eyelids automatically fluttered shut. When Jared's tongue slipped into her mouth, tasting of the sweet tea he had sipped earlier, she shuddered as a delicious shiver ran up her spine.

Sensations she had never felt before consumed her and when she felt his hands wrap around her middle, pulling her close to the fit of his hard body, she could have melted right where she stood. His assault of her mouth was deliberate, sensuous, unhurried. It was meant to tantalize and awaken every part of her and it did.

Then he deepened the kiss, taking it to another level as he continued to take her mouth slowly, thoroughly, passionately. A part of her wanted to pull back, but he was right. This was the perfect way to end the day. They had been attracted to each other from the first and to pretend otherwise would be a complete waste of time. And since this was the last time they'd spend together, they could at least have this moment.

So she hung in and continued to let him kiss her, finding exquisite pleasure in every moment that he did so. Then he changed the rhythm of their kiss as his tongue played seek and retreat with hers, making a whimper rumble from deep within her throat.

Heat throbbed within Jared as he continued to kiss Dana. Initially, he had meant for the kiss to be nothing more than a way of saying goodbye, to satisfy his curiosity and hunger, but the moment he tasted her sweetness he was helpless to do anything but sink in and savor.

He made sure his kiss was gentle but thorough as he relentlessly explored her mouth. His tongue dueled with hers in a slow sensuous motion and when she wound her arms around his neck and arched her body to the hard length of his, he was consumed with hot waves of desire. There was something about her that had his senses pulsating. Never before had he been this driven to devour anyone.

Moments later with a fevered moan, he lifted his mouth away from hers although he continued to track her lips with his tongue. "You're beautiful in every way that a woman can be, Dana," he whispered roughly against her ear, burying his face in her neck and placing a kiss there.

His compliment touched Dana's very core. No one had ever said such a thing to her. "Thank you."

"Don't thank me. It's the truth," he said, releasing her slowly and taking a step back. "And I want to thank you again for helping me out today."

"I want to thank you, as well. Like I said, your family is wonderful."

He nodded. There would be no reason to see her after today. He tried racking his brain for some excuse to drop by, but couldn't find one. He ran a frustrated hand across the back of his neck. No woman had ever had him this reluctant to say goodbye. He glanced around the room, stalling for time. "Where's Tom?" he asked, trying to prolong the time by even an additional second if he could.

"He's probably in my bed."

Damn lucky cat. Jared met her gaze and knew he should leave before he did something really crazy such as grabbing her and starting to kiss her again. "Goodbye, Dana."

"Goodbye, Jared."

"Take care of yourself." And with those final words he turned, opened the door and walked out of the house.

Three

Around ten the next morning, Jared walked into his parents' home. His nine o'clock court appointment had gotten canceled, which afforded him the opportunity to visit his mother and straighten out yesterday's misunderstanding.

"Mom! Dad!" he called out while walking through the living room to the kitchen.

"I'm out back," was his father's reply.

Jared opened the kitchen door and stepped onto the sun deck his father had built last year. He saw him busy at work putting a coat of polish on his classic Ford Mustang. "Good morning, Dad."

"Morning, son. What a nice surprise to see you on a Monday morning."

"I had a canceled court hearing this morning. Where is everyone?"

"Durango stayed over at Stone's place last night and Ian and Spencer are having breakfast with their cousins at Chase's Place. Quade had to fly out first thing this morning to return to D.C. and Reggie, I imagine went to work."

Jared nodded and glanced around. "I need to talk to Mom. Is she upstairs?"

His father sighed deeply. "No, she had a doctor's appointment this morning."

Jared frowned. "A doctor's appointment? Is anything wrong?"

His father shrugged. "I hope not, but you know your mother. If something is wrong then I'll be the last to know. She thinks if she tells me anything I'd worry myself to death. I wouldn't know about her appointment today if I hadn't heard the message the doctor's office left on the answering machine reminding her of it. Appears they found another lump during her checkup last week."

Jared's frown deepened. Three years ago his mother had been diagnosed with breast cancer and had undergone a series of chemo and radiation treatments before being given a clean bill of health.

"Mom's car is in the driveway so how did she get to the doctor's?"

"I offered to drive her but she had already made arrangements for your aunt Evelyn to take her. You know those two. They have been best friends for years."

Jared nodded. Everyone in the Westmoreland family knew how the two women who had been best friends since high school had ended up marrying the Westmoreland twins, becoming sisters-in-law. "Do you think it's anything serious?" he asked.

He couldn't help but remember how things were the last time. The cancer treatments had made his mother sicker than he'd ever remembered her being. He, his brothers and his dad had made the mistake of hovering over her as if she was an invalid. That hadn't helped matters, which was probably the reason she hadn't mentioned this doctor's appointment to any of them. They would have all shown up at the doctor's office with her today.

"To be honest, Jared, I was beginning to get concerned. I could tell she was worried, although she tried pretending that she wasn't. But then all that changed yesterday."

Jared raised a brow. "Yesterday? What happened yesterday?"

"You made her one extremely happy woman when you and Dana announced your engagement."

Jared opened his mouth to say that he and Dana hadn't exactly announced anything. His mother had assumed the wrong thing and jumped to conclusions.

"I think your engagement actually gave her a new lease on life, a determination to handle whatever it is the doctor is going to tell her today and for that I'm grateful. You know how depressed she got the last time she had to undergo all those treatments. If that's the verdict again, and God knows I hope it's not, she'll be more of a fighter because she knows she has an important day to look forward to."

"What day?"

"The day you and Dana will marry," James Westmoreland said smiling. "That's all she talked about last night and this morning. She likes Dana and thinks she'll make you a fine wife. So do I. You selected well, Jared, and your timing could not have been better. If there's a chance your mother's cancer has returned and she has to undergo more treatments, she'll do whatever she has to do to retain her health to help plan your wedding."

"My wedding?"

"Yes, your wedding. Thanks, Son, for giving your mother a reason to fight whatever we might be up against. She'll be able to handle anything now since she knows one of her sons is finally getting married and will eventually give her a grandchild."

Jared stood in stunned silence. One thing was clear—he couldn't tell his mother the truth about Dana now.

Dana glanced through her peephole and raised an arched brow. She and Jared had said their goodbyes yesterday, so why was he standing on her front porch at six o'clock in the afternoon?

She swallowed the knot in her throat and tried to stop the rapid beating of her heart. It didn't take much for her to remember the kiss they'd shared, a kiss she had thought about most of the day. Instead of concentrating on her work, her mind had been filled with memories of Jared Westmoreland and how well he could kiss, not wanting to think about what else he was probably an expert at doing.

She continued to study him through the peephole. He was dressed in his business suit, which meant he had probably come straight from the office. He looked coolly reserved, in control and professional. Yet at the same time he also looked devastatingly male, incredibly sexy and he was affecting her in that man-woman kind of way. Swallowing hard, she blew out a slow breath and told herself to get a grip as she opened the door.

"Jared?" She sounded breathless, even to her own ears and could only imagine how she might have sounded to his. And the way he was looking at her with those dark, intense eyes wasn't helping.

"Dana, I hate to bother you but I need to talk with you about something important."

Her eyes widened. Whatever he had to say sounded serious. "All right."

She stepped aside to let him in and closed the door behind him. "Can I get you something to drink?" she asked, leading him to her living room.

"No, I'm fine," Jared said, but feeling anything but fine. His conversation with his father had thrown a monkey wrench into what he'd planned to tell his mother. Out of the corner of his eye Jared saw Tom race from where he had been near the sofa to the vicinity of the kitchen.

Jared took the seat Dana offered him on the sofa and watched as she sat in the chair across from him. With everything on his mind, the last thing he needed was to notice the skirt and blouse she was wearing. But he hadn't been able to look away when she sat down and he caught a glimpse of thigh that her short skirt revealed. Nor could he dismiss the way her blouse hugged her breasts.

"Jared? You said you had something important you needed to discuss with me."

Her words reminded him of the reason he was there and he met her curious gaze. "I went to see my mother this morning to clear up the misunderstanding, but things didn't go the way I had intended. She wasn't home so I talked to my dad instead."

Dana nodded. "And you told him the truth."

"No."

"Oh?" Dana said, confused.

"There seems to be a problem," Jared said, knowing that he needed to tell her everything. He decided to start at the beginning.

"Three years ago my mother was diagnosed with breast cancer. The lump was removed and she went through eight weeks of both chemo and radiation. She had good days and bad days and my father, brothers and I saw just what a remarkable woman she was."

The sincerity in Jared's words touched Dana. She could imagine what Jared, his brothers and father had gone through. After spending time with his family yesterday, it was easy to see just how much Sarah West-moreland was adored by everyone.

"Anyway," Jared said, reclaiming Dana's attention, "I talked to Dad this morning and before I could tell him the truth about us, that there really wasn't an 'us,' he told me that the doctors found another lump in my mother's breast and if it's malignant, we might be talking about cancer treatments again."

"Oh, no," Dana whispered and immediately moved from her chair to sit next to Jared on the sofa. She reached out and touched his arm. "I'm sorry to hear that, Jared," she said in all sincerity.

He slowly stood and shoved his hands into his pockets. Her touch had elicited sensations throughout his body, sensations he didn't want to deal with right now. He had to stay focused.

"So am I," he said slowly. "However, knowing my mother, she will handle this like the fighter that she is.

But there's something I can do to make the fight a little easier for her."

"What?"

Jared met her gaze. "It's a crazy idea but at the moment I'd do anything for my mother, including lie."

Dana frowned, wondering what he would lie about. "Jared, what do you need to lie about?" she asked, rising from her seat to come stand in front of him.

His jaw muscles tightened and he briefly glanced away. When he met her gaze again, his eyes were intense and her breath caught at the tormented look she saw lodged there.

"Jared, what do you need to lie about?" she asked again.

He hesitated for a moment then said, "Us. My father made me realize just how happy my mother is, believing that I've finally decided to settle down and get married. Considering everything right now, I don't want to take that happiness away from her."

Reeling in confusion, Dana felt the need to take a step back. "What are you saying?" she asked, not sure she was following him.

"I have a proposal for you," he said, holding her gaze.

Dana swallowed. "What kind of a proposal?"

He gave her a not-so-easy smile. "That we continue to pretend we're engaged for a little while longer…for my mother's sake."

It would have been easier, Dana thought, if she had been sitting down instead of standing up. Nevertheless, the impact of Jared's words slammed into her.

She stared at him, looked for some sort of teasing glint in his gaze that indicated he was joking. But all she saw was an expression that said he was dead serious. Her mouth went dry and her heart began hammering in her chest. "Pretend we're engaged?" she finally found her voice to ask.

"Yes."

She inhaled slowly, deeply. "B-but we can't do that."

For several seconds he just looked at her. His shoulders straight, his gaze intent, clear. "Yes, we can. I never realized how much seeing at least one of her sons settling down meant to Mom. Now I do and I will do whatever I can to make her happy."

"Even get married?"

He frowned. "I hope I don't have to go that far, Dana. I think her believing I'm engaged will help at least until the worst part is over."

"And then?"

"Then I tell her things didn't work out between us and that we broke our engagement. It happens."

Deciding that standing wouldn't work, Dana sank back onto the sofa. "Trust me, I know all about broken engagements, Jared."

He sighed deeply. "I'm sorry. I know it's a lot to ask of you, considering your broken engagement with Luther, but I don't know what else to do."

The warmth in his gaze touched her. She wet her lips and leaned back in her seat, trying to absorb everything he'd told her. She couldn't help but admire him for his willingness to be a sacrificial lamb. He had no intention of ever getting married and had made that fact very clear. Knowing that, she was sure he didn't want to get involved in any of the trappings that led to marriage, either pretended or otherwise. Yet, for the love he had for his mother he would do what he felt he had to.

She lifted her chin and rubbed nervous hands against her skirt. "If I went along with you on this, Jared, just what would you expect of me?"

Jared moved to sit in the chair across from her. He was glad she was at least considering his proposal. "I've never been engaged before but you have. How were things with you and Cord?"

Dana sighed. "In the beginning I could actually see us spending the rest of our lives together. But now I have to admit that I wanted to marry him for all the wrong reasons. Love had nothing to do with it. He was handsome, successful—"

"And gay."

Dana raised a surprised eyebrow. "You knew?"

Jared shrugged. "I wasn't absolutely certain until I met you. The first thing that crossed my mind when you walked into my office was that no straight man in his right mind would let you slip through his fingers."

Dana couldn't help but smile at the compliment. "Thanks. I had no idea about Luther's sexual preference until recently. He came to see me and told me the truth. I can only appreciate that he broke our engagement when he did."

Jared nodded. "The two of you dated for over a year and you had no idea?"

Dana shook her head. "Not even a clue, although I realized afterward that the signs were all there but I ignored them."

Jared's brow furrowed. "What signs?"

Dana met his gaze. "Sex for instance."

A knot formed in Jared's throat. Silence grew between them—rather awkwardly, then he asked in a strained voice, "Sex?"

"Yes, sex. We decided that we wouldn't sleep together until after we were married."

Jared nodded. "Soo." He drew the word out, as if his mind was befuddled. "Whose idea was that?"

Dana bit her lip before answering. "It was Luther's idea and of course I went along with it since sex is overrated."

Jared's gaze was puzzled. It wasn't overrated in his book and he wondered how she could think such a thing. "Is it?"

"Yes."

She had him curious and he couldn't resist asking for clarification. "Why would you think that?"

She shrugged. "I'm not a virgin, Jared. I've had sex before and frankly I've never experienced anything worth losing sleep over."

He wondered who the men were who had disappointed her? He met her gaze, locked on it. "Maybe you haven't done it with the right person."

His softly decreed words spurred a hot little quiver that moved down the length of Dana's spine before blossoming out to every part of her body. She couldn't help wondering if a tumble between the sheets with him would make her think differently, then decided it was something she would never know. But still the thought caused a warm pool of heat to form in her belly.

She cleared her throat, needing to regain control of her senses. "Trust me, twice was enough. I can possibly understand the blunder in college, but I was involved with someone a few years ago and my opinion hasn't changed."

He leaned back in his chair, surprised that she was able to dismiss such a profound intimate act from her life just like that. "A few years ago? How far back was that?"

"Three years, closer to four."

Jared raised a dark eyebrow. "Are you saying that you haven't slept with a man in almost four years?" he asked, not sure if he had heard her correctly.

Dana lifted her chin, wondering how they had gotten on such a personal subject, but decided to answer anyway. "Yes, that's just what I'm saying."

Deciding she had given him enough information about herself, she said, "So tell me what things you expect us to do during this pretended engagement?"

He watched as she licked her lips again and wished it were his tongue at work instead of her own. And if that wasn't bad enough she crossed her legs and his gaze moved down the length of them, catching sight of the thigh he'd gotten a glimpse of earlier. His gut clenched when he thought of licking those legs and thighs.

Damn! He couldn't help but curse his bad luck. He was still way too attracted to her and the last thing he needed was a reason to spend more time in her company. In this situation, his mother's needs came before his own. But boy did he have needs and the enormity of those needs was hitting home—in this case right below his belt. He shifted in his seat to relieve the strain he felt behind his zipper. He could definitely use some sexual playtime and would've loved to suggest a purely physical relationship, with no emotions involved. But after her broken engagement, the last thing he wanted to do was take advantage of the situation by suggesting such a thing.

He cleared his throat. "What kinds of things did you and Cord do together?" He gave her a lopsided grin. "You've already told me about one particular activity the two of you didn't do."

Dana smoothed down her skirt. He watched as she then rolled one shoulder, which made his gaze move from her legs to her breasts. Suddenly he felt tension in his fingers. He would give just about anything to cross the room, lift her top, unhook her bra—if she was wearing one—and take his fingertips and graze her flesh before taking his mouth and latching on to a nipple and sucking—

"Luther and I went out a lot," she finally said, snatching back his focus. "We attended concerts, plays and parties. He was a sales representative with his company and often had to do a lot of socializing."

For several seconds Jared looked at her, thinking because of his clientele he often did a lot of socializing, as well. However, recently he'd cut back because of his workload. "We can do those same things. However, my mother is big on family gatherings and would expect us to also attend any. Can you handle that?"

Dana thought about how much she had enjoyed herself yesterday, almost too much. "Yes, I can handle that. Like I told you yesterday I think you have a wonderful family. But I'd hate deceiving them."

"It's for a good reason." A grin turned up the corners of his lips. "And I'd like to think that a pretended engagement with me wouldn't be so bad. I'm a pretty decent fellow."

Decency was the last thing on Dana's mind at the moment although she knew it shouldn't be. Heat was curling in her stomach just from staring at him. "How long do you think this pretended engagement will have to last?"

"That will depend on my mother's condition. If this is a false alarm, then we're only looking at a couple of weeks. But if we're looking at treatments, the last time they lasted for eight weeks. Will that be too long for you?"

Dana sighed. Any length of time would be too long as far as she was concerned. "No, umm, that would be fine."

Jared hated the uncertainty, the wariness he saw in her eyes but knew those emotions mirrored his own. He swallowed hard as he stood, shoving his hands in his pockets. "So, you're willing to keep on pretending to be my fiancée?"

Several tense minutes passed before Dana answered. She knew she might be asking for trouble, considering how attracted she was to him. But under the circumstances, there was no way she could turn him down. "Yes."

A relieved smile touched Jared's lips. He crossed the room and taking her hand he pulled her from her seat. "Thanks, Dana. Now I'm the one who's in your debt."

Having Jared in her debt stirred strange sensations in Dana's belly. She licked her dry lips, tried to smile and said teasingly, "That's okay. I won't demand anything that I don't think you'll be able to deliver." As far as she was concerned that left the options pretty wide-open.

Jared's gaze was drawn to Dana's lips; lips that were still moist from the recent sweep of her tongue. They stood so close that all he had to do was lean down and capture what he wanted most in his mouth and feast on it.

"So what's first?"

Her question made him lift a dark brow. He was about to say that a tongue-sucking kiss wouldn't be so bad, but changed his mind. "What's first?"

She smiled and he wondered if she knew what he'd been thinking, since his gaze was still glued to her lips. "Will your family need to see us together again anytime soon?"

He inhaled slowly. It's a good thing she'd asked. He had almost forgotten. "Yes. My brothers are remaining in town until Sunday, except for Quade. He had to get back to D.C. and flew out this morning. The folks are planning a cookout on Saturday evening."

Dana nodded. After spending time with Jared's family she knew his brother Quade worked for the Secret Service; Durango was a park ranger who lived in Montana; Ian was a ship's captain whose luxurious riverboat cruised the Mississippi River and whose home was in Memphis, and Spencer was a financial advisor, who lived in the quaint and quiet community of Sausalito, California. Jared and his youngest brother, Reggie, were the only ones living in the Atlanta area.

"Do they know what's going on with your mother's health?" she asked.

Jared shook his head. "No, and knowing Mom she'll tell us as little as possible and only what she thinks we need to know. It's her way of protecting us. But I'm going to tell them what I do know. We're meeting for dinner at Chase's Place in an hour, and I'll call Quade with details later tonight."

"Will you tell them the truth about us?"

Jared shook his head. "No. The less people who know the better. I won't take a chance on one of them letting something slip. I don't want to give my mother any reason not to think our engagement isn't the real thing."

Dana nodded. Suddenly, she remembered something. "The ring!"

Jared frowned. "What about it?" His gaze went to her left hand. He had noticed earlier that she wasn't wearing it.

"I don't have it anymore. I took it to a jeweler during my lunch hour. I needed the money to pay off some bills."

Jared rubbed the back of his neck. Although he hadn't much cared for seeing Cord's ring back on her finger, that ring symbolized their engagement. "Where did you take it?"

"Garbella Jewelers. Do you think they still have it?"

Jared inhaled as he checked his watch. Garbella was a well-known jeweler that was frequented by a lot of high-profile individuals. "Even if they do, chances are the shop is closed now. I'll check with them first thing tomorrow. If they still have it, I'll get it back."

"And if they don't?"

Jared inhaled again. "Then I'll get you another one."

"B-but your family saw *that* ring. They will think it's odd for me to start wearing a different one."

Jared nodded, knowing that was true. "Then I'll have to think of a good reason to tell them why I changed it."

Dana nodded. Whatever reason he came up with would have to be good. "All right."

He checked his watch again. "I need to leave if I'm going to be on time to meet my brothers for dinner."

Dana focused on putting one foot in front of the other as she walked him to the door. Concentrating on him was too mind-boggling.

They stopped when they reached her door. She lifted her gaze to his. His eyes appeared darker, the same color they had become right before he'd kissed her yesterday.

"I'll call you tomorrow," he said huskily. "Will there be a problem with me calling you at work?"

"No, there won't be a problem. Wait, I'll give you my business card."

Jared watched as she quickly crossed the room to a table, tempted to let out a low whistle. Heat flared through him as his gaze wandered down her hips, thighs and legs. He took a deep breath and released it. Dana looked particularly sexy in her short skirt. She definitely had all the right body parts for it.

"This has all of my contact information," she said, returning to where he was standing.

He took the card from her and felt her shiver when their hands touched. "Thanks."

She cleared her throat when he didn't make a move to leave. "Is there anything else, Jared?"

Her question made him realize that, yes, there definitely was something else on his mind. "It would be a good idea to seal our agreement and I think this way is more appropriate than a handshake."

Before she could gather her next breath, he leaned down, slanted his mouth across hers and captured her lips in his, tasting her the way he had wanted to since entering her home. He heard her purr, felt her nipples tighten against his chest, all the way through his jacket, which only made him intensify his hold on her mouth as his tongue continued to devour her.

His heart missed a beat with every stroke of his tongue and the multitude of sensations he encountered while kissing her washed over him, short-circuiting whatever functioning brain cells he needed in order to think straight. As if they had a mind of their own, his fingers inched downward to touch her thigh and to trace his fingertips along the hem of the short shirt that had been driving him mad for the past half hour. A warning flared in his mind that this woman was pure, unadulterated temptation.

He released her slowly and fought to control his breathing, his desire and his lust. The only word he could think of was—wow! Seducing Dana Rollins was not part of his proposal but...

"Do you think that was wise?" she asked in a low whisper.

His gaze went to her lips, lips that were still moist from his kiss. He liked the sight of them and a smile touched the corners of his mouth. "Yes, in all honesty, I think that was the smartest thing I've done all day."

Jared glanced around Chase's Place as he sipped his drink. The meeting with his brothers had gone rather well and everyone was in agreement that they wouldn't hover over their mother as they had the last time. They'd also agreed that Jared's engagement had been perfect timing, although they were glad it was him and not them.

"You okay?"

He glanced up and stared into the dark eyes of his cousin Dare. He and Dare were only months apart in age and had always shared a rather close relationship. "Yes, I'm fine, considering everything."

Dare took the chair across from him. "Durango told me and Chase what's going on with Aunt Sarah. You know the family is here if you need us for anything, but I know things are going to be fine."

Jared nodded as he rubbed a hand down his face. "God, I hope so. I don't even know how Mom's appointment went today. I stopped by earlier but it was like getting blood out of a turnip. The only thing she wanted to talk about was my engagement."

Dare chuckled. "Well, you have to admit that has given the family something to talk about. Who would have thought that you of all people would decide to finally tie the knot?"

Jared frowned. "It's just an engagement, Dare."

Dare nodded. "Yes, but unless you know something that I don't, most engagements are the prelude to a wedding. You'll be marrying Dana eventually."

Jared took another sip of his drink as he met Dare's gaze over the rim of his glass. One thing he'd learned as a successful attorney was knowing whom he could trust to keep their mouths closed and whom he couldn't.

"The engagement isn't real."

Dare straightened in his chair. "Excuse me?"

Jared spent the next ten minutes telling Dare the entire story, including how he and Dana had originally met.

"Damn, a pretended engagement. You know what

happened when Shelly and I tried pretending a court-ship. It became the real thing," Dare said, remembering that time.

Jared stared at Dare. "That won't happen to me. You know how I feel about marriage."

Dare chuckled. "Yeah, and you know how I felt about it, too. But I can't imagine not having Shelly in my life now."

"The two of you had a history. And then there was AJ."

Dare nodded when he thought of the son he hadn't known about until Shelly had returned to town after having been gone ten years. "But even with all that, Shelly and I had to get reacquainted, find ourselves all over again. It was only then that we discovered that we still loved each other."

Jared snorted. "At work I see marriage at its ugliest— when two people who'd vowed to love each other till death do them part, face each other in a judge's chamber with hatred in their eyes, wanting to strip the other bare of anything and everything."

He chuckled before continuing. "The man I'm representing in court tomorrow is fighting his soon-to-be ex-wife for custody of the dog."

Dare shook his head sadly. "Don't let what you see in your profession discolor your opinion of marriage, Jared."

Jared sighed deeply. "It already has, Dare. This thing with Dana is for Mom's sake and there's no way I'm going to forget it."

Four

Dana glanced up from her desk and smiled when Cybil walked in. "Good morning."

"Umm, I don't know how good it is when you find out your best friend has been keeping secrets."

Dana raised an arched brow. "Excuse me?"

Cybil frowned as she crossed the room to stand in front of Dana's desk. "I don't know whether you're excused or not. News of your engagement made the society column today," she said, waving a section of the *Atlanta Constitution* in front of Dana's eyes.

"What!" Dana snatched the paper from Cybil to read the article. "I didn't know."

Cybil lifted a confused brow as she crossed her arms over her chest. "What didn't you know? That you're engaged to one of Atlanta's most eligible bachelors or that news of it would appear in today's paper?"

Hearing the hurt in her best friend's voice, Dana lifted her gaze from the article to meet Cybil's gaze. "I can explain."

"Do tell."

Sighing deeply, Dana stood and crossed the room to close her door. She turned to Cybil. "You better sit for this."

It took a full twenty minutes to explain everything. It would have taken less time had her best friend not interrupted every five minutes to ask so many questions.

"Boy, this is unreal. The entire office is buzzing. I hope Jared gets you a different engagement ring. People will have a lot to say if they see you wearing the same ring Luther gave you."

Dana blinked. Jeez. She hadn't thought of that since she hadn't expected news of their engagement going public.

"Who do you think tipped off the papers?" Cybil asked.

"I'm not sure but it really doesn't matter at this point." Dana knew it had to have been someone in Jared's family, probably his mother. The article had been nicely written, letting all Atlanta know that one of the city's most sought-after bachelors had gotten engaged to Dana Rollins over the Easter weekend. "I wonder if Jared has seen it."

Cybil smiled that little knowing smile that meant her mind was churning and usually in the wrong direction. "My guess is that he has." She chuckled. "I can assure you that everyone in this office has."

Dana looked at her with a concerned expression on her face. "What are they saying?" She knew if anyone knew about the office gossip it was Cybil. Not that she participated in it but everyone knew that her two staff members, Mary Bonner and Helen Fisher, were Kessler Industries' biggest gossips.

"They're perplexed since no one noticed a ring on your finger. But I think most of them are happy for you considering your breakup with Luther. They've gone from pitying you to envying you, especially since you've snagged the handsome and wealthy Jared Westmoreland."

Cybil's smile suddenly faded before she continued. "But, once you and Jared break this engagement everyone will go back to feeling sorry for you again and wondering how you could let two good men get away." She met Dana's gaze. "I have a feeling I'm not going to like the way this will turn out, Dana."

Dana wasn't all that crazy about how things were going to turn out, either, but it was too late now. She had given Jared her word. She opened her mouth to tell Cybil not to worry, that in the end things would work out okay when the phone on her desk rang.

Grateful for a moment's reprieve she reached over and picked it up. "Hello?"

"Good morning, Dana."

Dana couldn't help the flutter that suddenly went through her midsection upon hearing the husky, sexy sound of Jared's voice. It would not have been so bad if she didn't also remember their kiss yesterday, not to mention the feel of his hand on her thigh. His kisses were getting bolder, hotter and more earth-shattering.

"Good morning, Jared." She glanced over at Cybil then quickly looked away when she saw how intently her friend was watching her.

"Have you seen this morning's paper?" he asked.

She considered his question and glanced over at Cybil again. This time she gave her a pointed look, one that requested privacy. However, Cybil just sat there, ignoring her request.

Dana sighed after giving Cybil a mean look and answered Jared's question. "Yes, I've seen it."

"I apologize for not letting you know about it, but I didn't know myself until I read it this morning. It seems my mother's happiness is getting the best of her."

"Yes, it appears that way, doesn't it," she responded, not knowing what else she could say. From his tone he didn't seem upset. In fact there appeared to be an underlying tenderness and warmth in his voice. Or was she just imagining things?

"Will you have lunch with me?" he asked.

"Lunch?"

"Yes, at Jenzen's."

Dana's eyes widened. Jenzen's was an exclusive restaurant in North Atlanta. She'd heard that reservations had to be made well in advance, oftentimes weeks. It was certainly not someplace that she frequented.

"Lunch is fine. Do you want me to meet you there?" she asked. She hated admitting it but she was looking forward to having lunch with him and a part of her chafed at the thought of that.

"No, I'll come pick you up. Is eleven-thirty okay?"

She checked her watch. She had a meeting that would be ending a few minutes before then. "Yes, that will be fine. I'll be standing in front of the building."

"Okay. I'm looking forward to seeing you again, Dana."

Dana hung up the phone, closed her eyes and bowed

her head wondering how Jared could set off so many emotions within her. Emotions she'd never felt before.

"You okay?"

Dana snatched her head up. She had forgotten Cybil was still in her office. "Yes, I'm fine. That was Jared."

Cybil smiled. "So I heard." She then stood. "Enjoy lunch but promise me one thing."

"What?"

"That you won't get yourself in too deep. I saw the expression on your face when you heard Jared's voice."

"And?"

"And I don't want to see you get hurt again."

Dana waved her hand in the air, dismissing Cybil's concerns. "Hey, I know the score between me and Jared. I'm merely doing him a favor."

"Some favor. I've seen him before and he's a hottie, every woman's fantasy. How far do you plan to take this pretended engagement? Will the two of you get intimate?"

Dana swallowed. "Intimate?"

Cybil grinned. "Yeah, you know, sleep together. Share the same pillow. Bump and grind. Have orgasms."

The scenario that suddenly played out in Dana's mind had her heart beating so fast she thought she would pass out. "Of course not!"

"Are you sure about that?"

Before Dana could respond Cybil opened the door and walked out.

Jared gazed across his desk at Sylvester Brewster, hating to admit that he hadn't looked forward to their meeting.

At twenty-eight, Sylvester was a well-known recording artist who toured the country performing songs that consistently hit the number-one spot on any billboard charts.

Unfortunately, in addition to his blockbuster hit records, Sylvester had this serious problem of wife-boredom. The man changed wives like he changed shirts, but one thing was always certain, when he cast one off to take on another he was extremely generous with the alimony.

Jared sighed deeply. It seemed Brewster was ready to dump the third Mrs. Brewster for wife number four. The only glitch in his plans was that his current wife wanted more alimony than Sylvester was willing to give her, which had his client fuming.

"I don't want to give her one penny more, Jared. Baby or no baby."

Jared lifted a brow. This was the first he'd heard of a baby. "Your wife is pregnant?"

"She says she is and could well be, but it makes no difference since it's not mine."

Jared's brow inched even higher. "Do you know that for certain?"

"Yes," Sylvester said with a frustrated sigh. Then lowering his voice as if the office might possibly be bugged, he whispered. "I'm sterile, man. As sterile as a new hospital on opening day. It's the result of a childhood illness. So if Jackie's claiming she's pregnant with my child then it's not mine."

Jared sighed deeply. "If what you're saying is true, that won't be hard to prove with a paternity test."

"It is true and nobody is going to try to lay a claim that I'm their baby's daddy."

Jared watched Sylvester pace around the room. "Should I be surprised if you remarry within hours of your divorce being final?" he asked, knowing that was usually the norm.

Sylvester stopped his pacing and met Jared's gaze and he actually saw deep hurt in the man's eyes. "No. I loved Jackie and wasn't involved with anyone else. With her there was never a dull moment, man, always excitement. She was something else. For the first time in my life I fell in love and look what happens. And that's what makes it so bad. Jackie refuses to level with me even after I told her I was sterile and there was no way that baby was mine. Now she's claiming that I'm the one who's lying." In anger, he hit his fist on the desk. "Women can't be trusted, man. I'll never marry again."

Jared was silent for several moments before he nodded, although not for one minute did he believe Brewster would keep that promise. Marriage was an addiction to Brewster, one Jared was glad he didn't have.

"I'll contact Jackie's attorney next week. I'm sorry things have come to this because I thought the two of you made a nice couple. But if you're certain she's been unfaithful then—"

"I'm certain. I don't have the name of the man she was involved with but there was an affair. Her pregnancy is proof enough."

Half an hour later, Jared had completed dictating information into his recorder for his secretary to transcribe. Standing, he walked over to the window and looked out. This was another morning that wasn't going well. First off the bat, while drinking his coffee and reading his newspaper, he had come across the article announcing his engagement to Dana.

Then he had arrived at Garbella Jewelers as soon as their doors had opened only to find that they had already sold Cord's ring. He had ended up purchasing another ring and was racking his brain for an excuse to give his family as to why Dana would no longer be wearing the original one. In his opinion, the only saving grace was that the one he'd purchased had a diamond that was twice as large and was closer to what he imagined Dana might like.

He sighed as he checked his watch. It was time to leave if he wanted to pick Dana up for lunch on time.

Dana.

She was becoming a major problem. He didn't consider his proposal a business arrangement. Otherwise he would have drawn up formal documents between them. She was merely doing him a favor. They had exchanged favors before so he knew she wouldn't go back on her word. But there were factors thrown in the equation that he hadn't counted on.

Like his strong attraction to her. And the dreams he'd been having.

Last night he had actually dreamed about her legs and thighs, in addition to other parts of her that he hadn't seen. In his dream, he had gotten all the way under that skirt she'd been wearing yesterday, first caressing the soft skin of her inner thigh before letting his fingers slide inside her damp heat. And then there were the kisses they had shared. His mouth tingled just remembering the taste of her on his tongue. Just thinking about her body parts and their kiss made his arousal thicken against his zipper.

For the life of him he couldn't understand this unusual brand of sexual chemistry. It wasn't as if he didn't come into contact with beautiful women. He'd once dated a former Miss Georgia for heaven's sakes. So what was there about Dana Rollins that had him counting the minutes, the seconds before he would see her again?

He hated admitting it, but the women he'd dated in the past were usually self-centered, aggressive and accustomed to getting their own way. But not Dana. She was strong-willed, but although he had witnessed her explosive temper the first day they'd met, he knew she was a kind person. She had cared enough about his mother's welfare to go along with his outrageous proposal of a fake engagement.

And speaking of his mother, Sarah Westmoreland definitely liked Dana. Yesterday she had gone so far as to suggest they have a short engagement and a June wedding. He had immediately burst a hole in her bubble by letting her know that was out of the question. But still, seeing the look of happiness on his mother's face made him realize that no matter what, this pretense of an engagement with Dana was worth it.

Jared rubbed the top of his head as he remembered his conversation with Dare last night. He'd meant what he told his cousin. Nothing, and he meant nothing, would develop between him and Dana, no matter how attracted he was to her. It wouldn't be the first time he was attracted to a woman and it wouldn't be the last.

His meeting with Sylvester had reaffirmed his conviction that marriage wasn't all that it was cracked up to be and he intended to enjoy his remaining days on this earth as a single man.

* * *

Whatever pep talk he'd given himself an hour earlier stood on shaky ground when lust took control of his body. A jolt of sexual awareness raced up his spine when he pulled up and saw Dana standing in front of her office building.

She was the model of professionalism with her upswept hairdo and two-piece navy-blue powerhouse suit. Her knee-length skirt was longer than the one she'd been wearing yesterday, thank goodness. He wasn't sure he'd been able to resist putting his hands on her bare thighs again.

She opened the car door and slipped inside. "Hi, Jared."

He swallowed. The air was suddenly charged with sexual energy. "Dana."

He watched as she snapped her seat belt in place and tried not to notice how her skirt inched up a little, exposing those thighs and long, shapely legs he had dreamed about. He breathed in the scent of her, a womanly fragrance that was just another sexy detail for his fantasies.

"Were you waiting long?" he asked, adjusting his sunglasses and trying to control the rapid beat of his pulse.

She smiled as she pressed back against the car's leather interior, unintentionally showing more leg and thigh. His heartbeat raced right along with his pulse. "No, I walked out a few minutes ago. Your timing was excellent."

His grip tightened on the steering wheel as he eased into traffic. There were cars everywhere, and he needed to focus on his driving and not on how firm Dana's breasts looked against her blouse. And heaven forbid he thought about her mouth and how it had parted under his yesterday, inviting him to deepen their kiss.

"Were you able to get the ring?"

He allowed his gaze to travel over to her when he came to a traffic light. "No. They had already sold it so I had to buy another one." He watched as that sexy mouth twisted into a frown.

"What will we tell your family?"

"That I liked this one better." Jared sighed deeply. That was the truth. He still didn't understand why it bothered him to see Cord's ring on her finger. Probably because he knew the whole story and felt she'd deserved better.

He glanced over at her again and watched as she pursed those same sexy lips and saw the frown lines appear between her prettily arched eyebrows. "It's going to have to sound convincing when you tell them that," she said.

He chuckled as he shifted his gaze from her to stare straight ahead. "I'm an attorney, remember. My job is to be able to convince people."

A grin spread over her face. "Yes, you're right. Sorry, I forgot." She was quiet for a few moments then said, "It was for the best anyway."

He lifted a brow. "What was?"

"Getting a different ring. That article in the newspaper this morning has my office buzzing and of course everyone wanted to see my ring. It didn't occur to me that had I kept Luther's ring they would have remembered it."

Jared blew out a breath. That hadn't occurred to him, either. "What did you tell them?"

"That it was being sized."

He nodded. "Sorry you were put in a sticky situation like that."

She shrugged. "No problem. I just hadn't expected that announcement to appear in the papers. I thought I only had to pretend this engagement for your family, not all Atlanta."

"Will that cause you problems?" he asked, seeing how deep the extent of their deceit was going.

"No, not as long as it doesn't cause you any problems."

Jared's forehead furrowed in confusion. "What kind of problems?" The car came to a stop at another traffic light and he glanced over at her.

"Your livelihood. You're one of Atlanta's most eligible bachelors. Being engaged takes you off the market for a while."

One corner of his mouth curved slightly. Being engaged would definitely change his life, but only temporarily. "Umm, I guess it does, but only for a short while." He held her gaze, studied it, looking for something, anything that would indicate she wished otherwise.

He let out a slow breath when he didn't see anything. He was glad that she understood that nothing could and would develop between them. Those hot and heavy kisses hadn't meant a thing and he didn't want her to get lust confused with love. Not that he thought that she would. But still, he had to be certain they were on the same page.

Their engagement was a game and nothing more.

* * *

Dana was very much aware of the man who sat across from her in the exclusive restaurant, and had been since he had picked her up for lunch. The twenty-minute ride had been taxing when all she could do was remember what Cybil had asked about their physical relationship.

The thought that Jared might expect them to become intimate was confusing and something she knew they should discuss. But she hadn't been able to bring it up. During the drive they had talked about several things but had played it safe and avoided mentioning their engagement. Instead they had discussed the weather, the new movies that had come out over the Easter weekend and Georgia's recent elections.

She wasn't surprised to learn that he lived in Country Club of the South, an affluent subdivision in North Atlanta, in the suburbs of Alpharetta. The houses were priced in the millions and a number of celebrities and sport entertainers lived there.

"You're quiet."

Dana glanced up and met Jared's dark gaze. He had been watching her. Something flickered in the depths of those eyes that made her catch her breath, made something unbearably hot flow through her veins. She picked up her coffee cup to break eye contact. Cybil had warned her not to get in too deep and she had assured her friend that she wouldn't. When she said it she had been sure, confident, but now all that assuredness was skating on thin ice. Jared Westmoreland was not a man to take lightly. He had made it clear in the car that their arrangement was temporary. She was smart enough to read between the lines. He'd been letting her know that he was not a man to whom any woman should give her heart. "Umm, I was just thinking about things," she finally said.

"Are you thinking of changing your mind about this?" he asked quietly.

She looked up and met his gaze again. Although she couldn't read his expression she really didn't have to. She knew how much keeping his mother happy meant to him and she couldn't help but admire the lengths he would go to for her. "No, I'm not, but there's something I think we do need to discuss," she said softly.

He nodded. "All right. What would you like to talk about?"

Dana sighed deeply. Even now she felt it, the hot, sultry passion that radiated between them, that was always there whenever they were together. It was that passion, the sexual chemistry, the strong attraction that let her know she was walking on dangerous ground with him.

"Our kisses," she said, almost in a whisper. But the sudden intensity of his expression let her know he had heard her.

"Our kisses?"

She looked down at her coffee cup again when she saw the desire that darkened his eyes. After pulling in a deep breath she met his eyes again. "Yes."

He tilted his head at an angle that seemed to make his gaze focus in on her. Only on her. "What about our kisses, Dana?"

Her palms were beginning to feel sweaty and her insides felt like molten liquid with his question. She wished she could respond by stating that she wanted more of them, but knew that would definitely be a wrong answer. She could barely handle the ones she had gotten so far.

She cleared her throat. "I—I don't want them to lead to other things."

He stared at her a moment then asked, "Does your definition of *other things* include what you and Cord never got around to doing?"

She bit her lip and tried not to look at him. "Yes."

After a brief pause he said, "Dana?"

The way he said her name only forced her to look at him. "Yes?"

"Why does the thought of making love to me bother you?" he asked softly.

She felt a tiny pull in the pit of her stomach at the silky timbre in his voice. The thought of making love to him didn't bother her but it did keep her constantly off balance and made her imagine some wild and purely wicked things. It also had her conscious of her sexual state more so than ever.

She hadn't slept with a man in almost four years. That fact hadn't bothered her before. It had seldom crossed her mind. Now it did. She was experiencing wants and desires for the first time and had a feeling that a sexual experience with Jared would obliterate her long-standing belief that sex was highly overrated. She knew to ask for a purely platonic relationship would not be realistic. After all, she was a woman and he was a man unlike any other she'd ever known. He had a way of making her feel attractive, wanted and desired.

The silence between them had stretched long enough

and she knew that he deserved an answer. "It doesn't bother me, Jared. It confuses me."

He didn't say anything for a long moment, and then he said, "Although I want to share a physical relationship with you, would it help to give you my word that I won't push you into doing anything you aren't ready for?"

She frowned. "That's just it, Jared. How will I know when I'm ready for anything? All of this is rather new to me."

"You'll know, Dana. You'll know better than anyone," he said softly. "I'd be telling a lie if I said I didn't want you. Even now, I want you so bad I ache with the thought of having you. I'm not Luther Cord. But since our engagement is not the real thing, I won't expect or assume anything. How far we take things will always be up to you."

"Thank you."

A warm shudder of awareness passed through them as well as an understanding and acceptance of their predicament. Jared recognized the depth of desire in her eyes although he knew she did not.

A part of him wanted to curse the two fools that had made her think that lovemaking wasn't worth losing sleep over. There was no doubt in his mind that if he ever made love to her, sleep wouldn't be involved. just constant pleasure, gratification and enjoyment all night long.

"And as far as the kisses," he said. "They can be dangerous but necessary. Engaged couples do kiss, so a certain degree of open affection will be expected. And although we don't have to kiss when we're alone, I enjoy kissing you and hope you enjoy kissing me, as well. But if you prefer that—"

"Kissing is fine," she interrupted. "Now that we have an understanding. Like you said earlier in the car, our pretended engagement is only temporary."

The drive back to her job was done mostly in silence. There really wasn't a whole lot left to be said. They understood each other and the situation they were in.

"Here's the new ring," he said, when he parked the car in front of her office building and she'd unsnapped her seat belt.

She accepted the gray velvet box and opened it up. He heard the gasp that escaped her lips and watched as she blinked then blew out a long whistle. "Wow!" She quickly looked over at him. "Don't you think this is a bit too much?" She took it out of the box and slipped it on her finger. It was a perfect fit.

Jared's mouth tilted into a smile. For some reason he liked seeing that ring on her finger instead of the one Luther had given her. "No. If I'm going to convince my family there was a good reason for me to change rings then seeing is believing. I'll just tell them that I saw this one and thought it would look better on your hand. They'll buy that story."

Dana nodded. Anyone would. Jared hadn't just given her a ring, he had given her a rock. It had to be the most beautiful ring she had ever seen and the design was unique. She knew it most have cost him a fortune. Of course she'd return it when their fake engagement was over. She held her hand out in front of her. "It's simply beautiful, Jared."

Smiling at her, Jared reached out and captured her

hand in his and brought it up to his lips. "I'm glad you like it."

Dana swallowed when he released her hand. Jared kissing her hand had been totally unexpected and she felt a sizzle all the way to her toes.

"Now I have a question for you," he said quietly before she could gather her wits.

"What?"

"Are those two people friends of yours? They have been standing there and staring at us ever since I pulled up."

Dana followed his gaze and saw Mary Bonner and Helen Fisher standing at the entrance of the building, pretending to be engaged in deep conversation. "They're co-workers, not friends, and two of the biggest gossips in the building."

A mischievous glint appeared in Jared's eyes. "Then how about if we gave them something to gossip about."

Dana smiled. She knew where he was coming from although she also knew his plan included another kiss. But they had said at lunch that engaged couples were expected to publicly display a certain degree of affection. And if she was totally honest, she wanted to feel his lips against hers again. "Okay."

Dana's breath hitched when Jared reached over and nearly pulled her out of the seat into his lap and captured her mouth with his. Her body respond instinctively. The kiss was soft, gentle, slow and hot. It was also thorough—so methodically complete that she felt blood race all the way down to her toes. Kiss number three was everything the last two had been and more. He was making her concentrate on his taste and the slow build-up of desire that was flowing through her. His tongue tangled with hers and she felt desire and urgency consuming him and overtaking her, as well. His hard shaft was pressed against her stomach and she knew for him to have gotten that aroused meant they were definitely putting on a show.

He slowly pulled back and she placed her hands against his muscled chest as she tried to restore her breathing to a normal pattern. Her insides felt like mush and heat, and an intensity she had never felt before settled smack between her legs.

"So…do you think that worked?" he asked, lowering his head to lightly taste the sides of her mouth while placing her back in her seat.

His breath was warm, his tongue moist and her control was steadily slipping. "Yes," she said, barely able to get the single word out. "I'm sure they won't be able to stop talking about us."

Five

Lanterns furnished a translucent glow to the Westmorelands' backyard. Chairs and tables were assembled in front of the lake and an area had been cleared for dancing. There was the mouthwatering smell of ribs and chicken cooking over charcoal, and a huge tent covered a number of tables that were loaded with all kinds of delectable foods.

In addition to Jared's brothers and cousins, former classmates and friends had been invited to the cookout. Dana sighed as she glanced around. She had been introduced to everyone as Jared's fiancée and when asked when the wedding would take place she would smile and say they hadn't set a date, but doubted it would be anytime that year.

"I can certainly see why Jared preferred this ring," Madison was saying, pulling Dana's attention back to the conversation around her. Jared had been right. His family had accepted the reason he'd given about the change in rings without question.

"It certainly makes a statement, doesn't it?" Tara inserted. "It's such a beautiful ring. The other one was really nice but this one is more like Jared."

Dana was about to ask Tara what she meant when Jared's mother appeared by her side smiling. "Are you enjoying yourself, Dana?"

Dana returned the older woman's smile. "Yes, and thanks for inviting me."

"No thanks needed. You're family now."

Dana nodded. She hated deceiving the older woman.

"You've been Jared's best-kept secret. Not once did he let on that he was seeing anyone seriously, in fact I assumed the opposite. For the longest time he claimed that he would never marry. That just goes to show what can happen when a person falls in love. And it's plain to see that he's fallen hard," Sarah added chuckling. "He hasn't taken his eyes off you all evening. I've never seen him this attentive to anyone before, and I'm supremely happy about it."

The thought crossed Dana's mind that continuing that "supreme happiness" was the only reason Jared had propositioned her to take part in this sham of an engagement. She wondered why that had her feeling oddly let down.

"What do you think of Jared's theater room?" Jayla asked a few minutes later when the topic had switched from Dana and Jared to the movies that were now playing at the theaters.

Dana looked puzzled, not knowing what Jayla was

talking about but knowing it was something that she should. "His theater room?"

Shelly grinned. "You mean he hasn't told you about all the remodeling he's done? When was the last time you were over at his place?"

Dana didn't know what to say. To say that she had never been to Jared's house would definitely seem odd. She opened her mouth to make something up when suddenly Jared materialized by her side. He leaned over and kissed whatever lie she was about to fabricate off her lips.

"Come dance with me, sweetheart." He glanced over at his mother and his female cousins. "Excuse us for a moment," he said before leading Dana off to the makeshift dance floor.

Taking her into his arms he looked down at her. Holding her close, he liked the feel of her breasts against his chest and the perfect fit of her body against his. "Was my rescue quick enough?" he asked, smiling and searching her face. He wished they were alone so he could end the torture and kiss her the way he'd thought of doing all evening. "I was on my way over to get you when I heard Jayla's question about my theater room."

Dana tilted her face up, and chuckled quietly. "Yes, you were quick enough. It would have seemed awfully odd for me not to know about your house. Is there something I should know about this room so when the next person asks I can be prepared?"

Jared lightly skimmed his fingers down her bare arm. He felt her shiver and liked the fact that he had caused it. But then, she was causing things to happen to him as well—like the unbearable ache that was building in his groin. He wanted her, and with their bodies so close, there was no way she wasn't aware of his aroused state. "I like watching old movies and I've installed a state-of-the-art home theater system, the latest in plasma technology. The sound system is three times clearer than in a movie theater." In truth, he didn't want to talk about his theater room. What he really wanted to do was nudge Dana's body even closer to his, latch on to her mouth, ignore everyone around them as he kissed her crazy.

Dana smiled up at him. "Umm, I'm impressed."

It was on the tip of his tongue to tell her that besides being impressed she was also hot. Her heat was burning him, further arousing him and making him want her even more. He had to give her a lot of credit. She knew how to make a statement in anything and everything she put on her body. Tonight she was wearing a V-neck green dress that stopped just above her knees. The way the dress hugged her curves showed just what a small waist and well-toned bottom she had. Her outfit had been murdering his senses ever since he had picked her up and was still killing them. He stifled a groan. Dana Rollins was subtle, but provocatively sexy.

"I think it's time you visited my home so you won't be left in the lurch again. I'd love to fix dinner for you at my place," he said, leaning down and caressing her lips with his. He looked for any reason to kiss her and didn't mind performing for an audience. At least that's what he tried to convince himself. But he knew he wasn't performing, liking the feel of her mouth against his. He couldn't wait to get her alone.

She gave a soft laugh as she gazed up at him. "Can you cook?"

He grinned. He was on a low simmer even now. "Yes. So what about this weekend?"

Her smile faltered. "I'll be going away this weekend, to Brunswick. Saturday is my mother's birthday and I want to put flowers on her grave."

His gaze focused on her eyes and he saw that the sparkle had gone. He had also heard the sadness in her voice and knew going back to where her parents were buried would be hard on her. "My thoughts will be with you this weekend," he said softly. He pulled her close against him. Moments later he asked, "What about dinner at my place the week after you return?"

She looked up at him and smiled. Knowing he would be thinking of her this weekend touched her. "I'd love to," she said just as the music ended.

It was close to one in the morning when Jared returned Dana to her home. Although it was late she invited him in for coffee and, not surprisingly, he accepted. They had shared several slow dances, and each time she had been fully aware of his aroused state, and just as certain he had been aware of hers. At one point, he had guided her to a darkened area of the yard and had been seconds away from kissing her when Durango had cut in. She had seen the murderous look in Jared's eyes, but his brother had merely laughed it off. But now she was home, he was here with her and they were alone.

As soon as the door closed behind him, he pulled her into his arms and she went willingly, wanting his kiss as much as he wanted to give it. The mating of their mouths seemed endless, his tongue was torture of the most brazen kind.

Lust ignited within Jared with the way Dana's body seemed to dissolve into his, and at that moment he had to touch her, taste her, further stroke the heat building between them. He stroked his palms over her shoulders and upper arms, hearing the sound of her whimpering and moaning in his mouth. He continued to kiss her hungrily, greedily, needing her taste as much as he needed his next breath. And she clung to him, kissing him in return, sending him more over the edge than he already was.

Moments later he pulled back before he was tempted to sweep Dana into his arms, take her into the bedroom and make love to her all night long.

He met her gaze. Saw the heated look in her eyes and his entire body immediately reacted. Leaning forward he kissed the bare skin of her neck, liking the way it tasted, tempted to taste her all over. Beneath his tongue he felt her shiver, felt himself get harder and knew if he didn't stop what he was doing, temptation would get the best of him.

But he didn't want to stop. He wanted her with an intensity that almost took his breath away and had him working on minimum control and very little else.

With much effort he leaned away to look at her. He would give anything to take that dress off her body and get her naked. Then he would take his hands and cup her breasts and after driving her wild with his tongue on her nipples he would get on his knees and kiss a path all the way down her body until he reached—

"Jared?"

Her soft whisper interrupted his thoughts. "Yes?" he responded, his voice husky, thick with sexual need.

"I think you should leave now."

He took a deep breath, losing his calm as he'd lost his control. He knew that asking him to leave was her way of letting him know that she wasn't ready for the bedroom yet, and if they continued at this pace he would definitely take her there. He heard her words but still a part of him—that part that wanted her, needed her—felt inclined to push.

"You want me, Dana. I can see it in your eyes. I can hear it in your breathing. I can taste it in your kiss. Why deny what you want?"

She placed her fingers to his lips. "Yes, I want you, but I can't become involved in a meaningless affair, Jared. As soon as your mother is given a clean bill of health you'll be ready to break this fake engagement and walk away. Do you deny that?"

She stared at him, waiting for an answer, and he gave her the only one that he could give. "No, I don't deny it."

"Then Counselor, not giving in to my desires is the right thing," she said, taking a step back away from him.

He frowned. "I can't give you more, Dana," he said, annoyed with the circumstances surrounding them.

"And I haven't asked you to give me more, Jared. But then you shouldn't expect me to give you more than I can, either."

Exasperated, he rubbed a hand down his face. "Why make things complicated?" he asked, clearly frustrated.

"That's the last thing I want. In fact I'm trying not to complicate things. If I thought for one minute that I could handle an affair with you then we would be in my bedroom right now, getting it on. But I can't," she said feeling just as frustrated as she knew he was.

Jared sighed and reached out and pulled her tensed body into his arms. "Look, I'm sorry. I didn't mean to push, especially when I said that I wouldn't. But I want you in a way that I shouldn't. I don't think I've ever wanted a woman as much as I want you."

Jared was consumed by a need to do nothing but hold her. He didn't know how long he could hang on with their pretense but knew he had to see it through. Somehow he needed to build an immunity against the wants and desires that overtook him whenever he was within ten feet of her.

Moments later, he pulled back and looked at her. "I'll be out of town this week and won't be returning until late Friday night. When are you leaving town?"

"Early Saturday morning. It's about a seven-hour drive because I like to take the scenic route and spend the night on one of the Sea Islands."

He draped an arm casually around her shoulders. "Which one?"

"Jekyll Island. It's beautiful and close to Brunswick. My parents used to take me camping there each year."

"When will you be back?"

"Probably late Sunday evening."

Jared nodded. If she was leaving early Saturday morning that meant he wouldn't see her again until she returned. He leaned down and gently kissed her once more. And now since they were alone, he nudged her body closer, liking the feel of his palms on her back-side. He felt the tips of her breasts harden against his chest and reacted by pressing his erection low against her belly. The sensations spreading through him were relentless and fierce, and he plunged his tongue even deeper into her mouth, tasting her, devouring her, driving them both crazy with desire. "Miss me while I'm gone," he whispered, when he finally released her mouth. He knew he had to leave. If he stayed one minute longer, he wouldn't be able to control his actions. "Goodnight, Dana."

He then opened the door, stepped out and closed it quietly behind him.

Dana sighed deeply and leaned back against the door, missing Jared already. She had to be realistic about her pretended engagement or else she would fall head over heels in love with him. And that was something she could not and would not let happen.

Two hours later Jared was in his bed wide awake, flat on his back and staring up at the ceiling. Maybe he was moving too fast with Dana and should slow down. He had a reputation for being an in-control kind of guy, but lately he'd been losing control whenever it came to her.

He wished there was some way he could close his mind and thoughts to wanting and desiring her so much but was finding it impossible. He never intended for their pretended engagement to lead to a brief affair. It was hard getting his mind back in focus, and nearly impossible to remember that their relationship wasn't real.

Even his brothers and cousins had teased him relent-lessly tonight about how hard he had fallen for her. And on top of that, his father had taken him aside and asked if he was sure he could wait another year for a wedding.

Jeez. Was it blatantly obvious to everyone just how much he wanted her? And for a while tonight, while introducing her to neighbors and friends, he had actually considered Dana his.

His.

His heart slammed against his ribs at the thought of anything so foolish. He'd never considered a woman his because he didn't want any woman to consider him hers. He was only interested in the physical side of a relationship and not the emotional. He had enough of emotional entanglements with the cases he handled.

Crossing the room to his dresser, he opened a drawer and pulled out a pair of swimming trunks. Removing his pajamas bottoms he eased the trunks over his still aroused body thinking that a swim in the pool might cool him off and help calm his mind.

It was almost dawn when Jared returned to his bedroom. His body was exhausted but his mind still swam with thoughts of Dana.

The next few days were busy for Dana. The buzz around the office about her engagement had settled down, however, word had quickly spread about the rock she was wearing on her finger. More than once, a curious co-worker had stopped by her office to get a look at it. Tara had been right. Jared certainly knew how to make a statement. It was just too bad the statement he was making was not true.

On Tuesday morning, she got an unexpected call from Jared's mother.

"Mrs. Westmoreland, this is a pleasant surprise," she said smiling, and meaning every word. The more she was around the older woman, the more she liked her, mainly because she reminded her a lot of her own mother—friendly, outgoing and devoted to her family.

"Dana, how are you dear? I was wondering if you could join me for lunch at Chase's Place?"

Dana lifted an eyebrow as she checked her watch. "Sure. Would noon be fine?"

"It would be perfect. Do you know how to get there or do you need directions?"

Dana chuckled. "Yes, I know how to get there. It's a favorite for a lot of my co-workers. I've even eaten there a couple of times myself. The food is fantastic."

"Yes it is. Chase still uses some of the Westmoreland family's secret recipes."

A few hours later as Dana drove to Chase's Place, she couldn't help but think about Jared. He had left a message on her answering machine last night to let her know where he'd gone, which was definitely information a fiancée should know should anyone ask. He'd even left the number where he could be reached should she need him.

But she didn't need him.

Unfortunately, she had to remind herself of that very thing pretty often these days. She shouldn't make more of what was going on between them than there really was. Even he had admitted that when this sham was no longer needed he would walk away without a backwards glance.

So why don't you just enjoy whatever moments you have with him? an inner voice screamed. *Why does*

*there have to be regrets after goodbyes? You may not
want to fall in love with him but you're halfway there
already. Admit it.*

A lump formed in Dana's throat. She refused to admit anything. Hadn't she learned a cruel lesson about depending on others for her happiness? First there was the loss of her parents and then Matt and Luther, two men who had walked into her life and then walked out…just like Jared intended to do.

She'd known the score going in so, unlike the others, when he did his disappearing act she would be ready.

Dana saw Jared's mother sitting at a table the moment she entered the restaurant. She thought Sarah Westmoreland was a beautiful woman at fifty-seven with short black hair she wore in an Afro. She had dark brown eyes, dimples in both cheeks and a medium-size figure. Her smile was always gracious and sincere and Dana knew she wouldn't just be a mother-in-law to her sons' wives, she'd be like a second mother.

"Mrs. Westmoreland," Dana said as she approached the table.

"Dana, it's good seeing you again," the older woman said, standing and giving her a huge hug. From the first, Dana had decided that Jared's mother was a warm, loving person. And there was so much excitement in the older woman's voice on seeing her that no one would think they had just seen each other on Saturday, which was only three days ago.

"And it's good seeing you, as well," Dana responded, thinking she could get used to all the love and affection the woman generated.

Once they took their seats Mrs. Westmoreland smiled and said, "How are things going at work? Jared mentioned you're a landscape architect. That sounds like a real interesting profession."

Dana smiled. "It is. My parents owned a nursery so I got interested in trees, plants and shrubs fairly early in life." She paused while the waitress gave them glasses of water and their menus. Then she continued. "A lot of people don't understand the involvement of a landscape architect whenever a building is constructed. My job is to make sure the outside area is not only functional but also beautiful and compatible with the natural environment. "

Sarah Westmoreland nodded. A sad look then appeared in her eyes. "Jared told me about your parents' passing. That must have been devastating for you."

Dana nodded. "Yes, it was. I was the only child and was very close to my parents. Their deaths left me without any family."

Sarah smiled warmly as she reached out and covered Dana's hand. "Well, all that's changed. Like I told you the other night, the Westmorelands are your family now and I want you to feel like a part of us."

"Thanks." Dana felt a deep lump in her throat. She hated deceiving Jared's family, although she knew it was being done for a good reason. Dana looked down to study her menu. There was no way she could look at Mrs. Westmoreland right now.

"So, dear, have your heard from Jared since he's been gone?"

Dana glanced up. At least her answer wouldn't be a total lie. There was no reason Mrs. Westmoreland needed to know that, although Jared had called, she hadn't actually spoken with him. "Yes, he called last night."

"I'm sure that he's missing you."

Dana smiled. She doubted Jared was missing her but she definitely was missing him, although she didn't want to. She spent her days trying not to think about him, but found herself doing it anyway.

Dana took another sip of her water and decided to shift the topic off her and Jared. "So, how have you been?" she asked the older woman.

Sarah smiled. "I'm fine. I'm sure Jared told you that I had breast cancer a few years ago and that recently the doctor found another lump. But there's a chance it's nothing more than fatty tissue. I'm having it removed in two weeks and then we'll know the results. Whatever it is, I'll deal with it. I'd be the first to admit chemo and radiation were hard on me, but if I have to go through them again, then I will. I'm a fighter, Dana. My family gives me a lot to fight for. And I'm looking forward to the day when I become a grandmother," she said excitedly. "Jared told me that the two of you wanted children."

Dana inwardly thought that that was a lot for Jared to have said, considering they had never discussed children, not that they really planned on having any together.

At that moment the waitress walked up to take their orders and Dana was grateful for her timely arrival. A pretended engagement was bad enough. The last thing she needed to think about was having Jared's baby.

Six

On Wednesday evening after feeding Tom, Dana curled up in her favorite chair to read and relax. It had been a hectic day. One of her clients had been difficult, upset that the city's ordinances would keep him from constructing a huge man-made waterfall on the property where he planned to erect his company's building.

Not wanting to think about the problems that had plagued her that day any longer, she switched her thoughts to the lunch she'd shared with Jared's mother yesterday. Afterward she felt a special bond toward the woman that she shouldn't feel and didn't deserve. She wondered what his family would think when they ended their engagement, which just might be two weeks from now if his mother's test indicated her lump was benign.

She glanced up from her book when she heard the

sound of the doorbell. It was barely six o'clock and she wasn't expecting anyone. Cybil and Ben had decided to take the week off to visit his brother in Tennessee.

The moment she glanced out of the peephole, her heart stopped. It was Jared. She hadn't expected him back until late Friday. Taking a deep breath she slowly opened the door. "Jared, you're back."

He leaned in the doorway, and they stared at each other for a moment before he said, "Yes, I finished up earlier than expected but I haven't made it home yet. I thought I would drop by here first."

Dana was curious why he would come by her place before going home. The only thing she could think of was that maybe he'd heard about her having lunch with his mother and wanted an update. But then he could have called her to get that information. She cocked her head and looked at him. He stood in front of her door with such a strong, manly presence, she barely found her voice to say, "Come on in."

Jared sighed deeply as soon as he walked into Dana's home and the door closed behind him. Her expression had indicated that she was surprised that he had come straight from the airport. Hell, he was surprised himself. He had missed her like crazy and the only thing he could think of was that when the plane landed he had to see her.

He looked at her, thinking that the late-afternoon sun that shone through the living-room window seemed to make Dana all aglow. He could only stand there and stare at her, thinking just how beautiful she looked while wearing a pair of shorts and a T-shirt that said I'm Yours. Boy did he wish. Every fiber in his body stirred at the thought.

Being alone with her was causing his brain to short-circuit and he felt heat slowly move around in his belly. He breathed in her womanly scent and watched all the questions that were forming in the depths of her dark eyes.

"Did you miss me?" he finally asked. Needing to know. Wanting to know. Hoping like hell that she did and at the same time not understanding why he cared if she had or hadn't.

Dana tried shoving aside the shiver that raced up her body. Yes, she had missed him. Damn him for asking. It didn't take much to recall what happened the last time they were together, in this very same room—the heated kiss that had had her tasting him for days afterward. She could lie to him and say that she hadn't missed him or she could tell the truth.

But first, before she would admit to anything, she had a question of her own. "Did *you* miss me?"

Slow amusement lit the depths of Jared's dark eyes at the way Dana had turned the tables so he would be answering her question instead of her answering his. He smiled. She was about to get an answer he doubted she was ready for. But she *had* asked.

"Oh, yeah, I missed you. I thought about you every day, although I didn't want to. I also dreamed about you every night, and in those dreams I did all those things that you aren't ready for me to do. I made you realize how wonderful it can be when two people—the right two people—make love."

He crossed his arms over his chest and after a short moment of silence he said, "Okay, I've answered your question so how about answering mine. Did you miss me?"

They stood facing each other, both intently aware that something had shifted between them. They were doing more than wavering on the edge; they were hanging on for dear life. The chemistry between them was more powerful than ever, explosive, and deliriously potent. At that very moment, Dana wondered what could be the worst thing to happen if she told him she *had* missed him, *and* with the same intensity he'd claimed and so vividly stated.

She had also dreamed about him each night and each time he had invaded her sleep he had made love to her. In the deep unconsciousness of her mind she had easily and willingly given everything to him and he had pleasured her in ways she could only imagine. She had felt safe in knowing that when she awoke, she could face reality. But a secret part of her yearned to see how close her dreams were to the real thing. Could he actually make her reach an orgasm that many times? Even reaching one would be a first for her.

"Dana?"

He reclaimed her attention. "Yes?"

"I asked if you missed me," he said softly.

Yes, he had. And she would try to answer him, although not in the same depth that he'd done. "Yes, I missed you. And I dreamed about you, too." She watched as his nostrils flared and she heard his quick intake of breath.

He slowly uncrossed his arms. "And in these dreams…"

Dana tilted her head and looked at him. "That's for me to know."

A smile touched the corners of his lips as he took a couple of steps toward her. "And for me to find out?"

She held his gaze. "I doubt that you can."

Jared lifted a dark eyebrow and Dana immediately knew her mistake. She had given him a challenge.

She couldn't help but let her gaze lower to his fly and felt herself stirred by what she saw. He was an unashamed, very aroused man. She swallowed deeply and snatched her gaze back to his face. She tried desperately to remember the last conversation they'd had here in this house. Hadn't it been a mere five days ago? But for the life of her, her mind was getting fuzzy, heated and filled with more desire than she could handle.

"I thought we decided not to complicate things," she said, trying to hold on to her sanity as much as she could.

Another smile curved his lips. "Finding out just what kind of dreams you had is the most uncomplicated thing I'll ever do. Uncomplicated and very satisfying for the both of us."

Dana saw the look of intent in his eyes and took a step back. She folded her arms beneath her breasts. "I won't sleep with you, Jared."

She saw him lift another eyebrow as he regarded her. She realized too late that she had made another mistake because she had intentionally given him another challenge.

"And I told you, Dana, that I won't push you into doing anything you aren't ready for."

She frowned slightly. "And what do you think you're doing now if not pushing."

He lifted a shoulder in a shrug. "Making an attempt

to destroy your theory that sex is overrated. But, I don't have to sleep with you to do that."

"You don't?"

"No."

Dana swallowed, saw the intensity in his gaze. She believed him. Now she understood why he was one of the most successful attorneys in Atlanta. "You're smooth," she decided to say, meaning every word. He was using every weapon at his disposal to break down her defenses. There was the huskiness of his voice, the look of heated desire in his eyes and his very obviously aroused body. Even his stance was provocatively sexy.

"I'm also thorough, Dana."

She swallowed again and wondered why on earth was he making this difficult? But then another part of her couldn't help but be curious. Could he really prove that sex wasn't overrated without sleeping with her? What would he do to prove it? Just thinking about what approach he might use stirred her up. Boy, was she tempted to find out. And his penetrating stare wasn't helping matters. He was definitely rattling her resolve and kicking good common sense straight out the window.

"You once asked me how you would know when you were ready for me, Dana," he said softly, reclaiming her attention—not that he'd fully lost it. "You might not be ready to sleep with me but I think you're ready for this. What do you think?"

Dana sighed. How could she know if she was ready for *this,* when she didn't have a clue what *this* entailed. But she did know that whatever it was, it would be something she would regret not experiencing if she sent him away.

Her gaze swept over him thoroughly one more time before she made her decision. "I think you might be right."

He nodded slowly. "It's your call."

There was considerable silence. Then finally, Dana retraced the distance between them and stood before him, met his gaze, held it. Everything inside of her stirred with heated lust. "Then I'm making it."

Jared smiled. He liked everything about her—her smile, her body, her mind. He shook his head. Forget about what he liked. It was time to focus on what he wanted. Dana Rollins was one hell of a seductive woman.

And he wanted her.

He had told her they wouldn't sleep together, but he intended to drive her as far over the edge as she could go. "Do you trust me, Dana?"

She nodded, realizing what he was asking and why he was asking it. She stared deeply into his eyes when she answered. "Yes, I trust you."

"Good." And then without wasting any more time, he swept her into his arms and quickly moved in the direction of her bedroom.

"But—but you said we wouldn't sleep together."

He gazed down at her. "We're not. We're going to play a game."

She clutched the front of his jacket to hold on to since he was walking so fast. "A game?"

"Yeah. My version of Red Light, Green Light."

"Oh."

Jared smiled thinking of the possibilities as he placed her on her bed. He was glad Tom was nowhere around, and just to make sure the cat didn't show up later, Jared walked over to the bedroom door and closed it.

He sighed when he turned back to Dana and saw the look of uncertainty in her eyes. He had to remain composed for both their sakes. "Do you want to change your mind about this?" he asked softly, respecting her doubts and fears. It wasn't about taking care of his body's needs but rather, introducing her to how wonderful things could be between a man and a woman.

She met his gaze as she settled back in the bed. He tried not to concentrate on her legs and thighs and was finding it near impossible not to. "No, I don't want to change my mind, Jared."

"Are you sure?"

She nodded. "Yes."

He moved away from the door and came to stand by the foot of the bed. "Then let me tell you about this game," he said, removing his jacket and tossing it on a chair in her room. "The light will always be green, letting me know it's okay to move forward. But at any time you feel rushed, overwhelmed or want me to stop, all you have to say is red light. Understand?"

She slowly nodded, although at the moment the only thing she fully understood was that he looked good standing at the foot of her bed, especially in his extremely aroused state. She wondered what he would be getting out of this since they wouldn't be sleeping together.

He must have read the questions in her eyes. "This isn't about me, Dana. It's about you. I can handle things and how I do so is only for me to know."

"And for me to find out?"

Jared laughed. The first real good laugh he'd had in a long time. "Yes, maybe one day."

He moved slowly toward the bed and braced one knee on the mattress. He pulled her into his arms and whispered, "Green light." Bending his head he captured her lips. The moment his tongue slid inside her mouth, heat consumed him in a way it never had before. It was hard to believe that he could want a woman this badly, with this much intensity and desire. He kissed her the same way he had dreamed about and was thrilled that she was returning his kiss with equal fire, with an urgency that only made him want her even more.

Suddenly, she broke off their kiss. "Red light," she said breathlessly, barely able to get the words out.

He stopped kissing her and met her gaze. "I needed to breathe," she explained. He didn't say anything but continued to look at her. He watched as she took slow uneven breaths and licked her lips. Moments later she said softly, "Green light."

He was ready. He captured her mouth again in his and pulled her up against his erection, wanting her to not only see but to feel what she did to him. He palmed her bottom, and then moved his hand to stroke her thighs. He slowly shifted his hand to the area between her legs, wanting to touch her and not intending for a pair of shorts to stand in his way.

He pulled back. "Red light," he said and smiled when he heard Dana whimper in protest. He met her gaze. "May I remove your shorts and T-shirt?"

Dana stared at him for a moment, melted under his seductive gaze and whispered, "Green light."

Jared's breathing almost stopped. She had given him

the go-ahead and he intended to take it to the max. Leaning toward her, he whipped the T-shirt over her head and tossed it across the room, leaving her in a black lace bra. His mouth itched, his tongue thickened at the thought of how her breasts might look. Whether he got to find out or not would be her decision. But he was a man who was used to compromising. If she wanted to keep her scrap-of-nothing bra on, he could taste her breasts without taking anything off.

He shifted his attention to her shorts, reached out and when she lifted her hips he slowly eased them down her legs to reveal black lace panties. He'd never appreciated black lace so much until now. He tossed her shorts aside to join her T-shirt. Then on his knees he leaned over her and gently lifted her bra to uncover her breasts. Dana whimpered, but didn't protest. At that moment he couldn't have looked away even if someone yelled "Fire." He had to actually fight to control his breathing. She had the most beautiful, luscious pair of breasts he had ever seen on a woman. They were full and firm.

He met her gaze. She was looking at him just as hard as he was looking at her. "The light still green?" he asked softly, in a shuddering breath.

"Yes."

One day he would show her his undying gratitude. But for now…he reached out and cupped her breasts, tracing a fingertip around the dark tip of her nipple, first one and then the other. He heard her sharp intake of breath and it heated him more. Leaning over he captured a nipple gently between his teeth and holding it captive he used his tongue to make her as hot as he was.

Dana curled her hand into a fist as feelings she had

never encountered before slammed through her. She could barely stay on the bed, with the sensations Jared was evoking heightening her gratification to a level of pleasure she hadn't thought existed. He was taking one breast, and then the other, tugging at a nipple drawing them into his mouth, torturing them with his tongue.

She closed her eyes, feeling herself being pulled under the most sensual haze ever. A moan escaped her throat. She heard it and knew he heard it, as well. But he didn't stop doing what he was doing. She had dreamed about him doing this to her but her dreams weren't anything like the real thing.

When she felt him release her nipples she opened her eyes and met his heated gaze. "Light's still green?" he asked huskily.

She nodded. She couldn't speak. "Then lie back for me," he requested softly.

She did what he asked and her stomach clenched when he began tracing a trail of kisses from her breasts all the way to her navel. And if that wasn't bad enough, she felt his fingers easing inside her panties, setting off a deep throb between her legs. Any thoughts of resisting were forgotten. She had given him the green light to do as he pleased; and it seemed his most fervent desire was pleasing her.

Jared felt her heat. He smelled her scent and his erection got harder, increased in length. He ignored the tremendous ache in his groin as he forced his mind to concentrate on Dana. He eased his finger inside her panties and found her wet heat.

He let his fingertips have their way and Dana automatically parted her legs for him. Then he went to work, stroking her back and forth, over and over again, glorying in the sounds of her moans, the sensuous catch in her breath, her purrs, the way she groaned his name.

Without missing a beat with his fingers, he eased his mouth away from her navel and back to her lips, nipping at them, tracing his tongue from corner to corner. And then he went into her mouth with an urgency that was earth-shattering, increasing the stroking of his fingers, feeling her getting wetter, hotter, slicker. She couldn't stay still and wiggled her bottom and pushed up against his fingers.

"Jared!"

And then it happened. He felt it and continued what he was doing but lifted his head to look at her. He thought that she was beautiful while having an orgasm and knew at that moment he would want to see her in the throes of passion for the rest of his days.

For the rest of his days. He blinked, quickly pushed that thought away and wondered what craziness would make him even think such a thing. Dana had no place in his future. No woman did. But knowing that couldn't keep him from reaching out and pulling her into his arms and kissing the sweet taste of sweat from her forehead as her spasms slowly subsided.

He felt his erection throbbing and he fought back his own need for release. This was her time and as far as he was concerned, it was only the beginning. One day his time would come. Meanwhile...

He brought his head down and captured her mouth. Needing the taste of her with an urgency that he didn't quite understand. The kiss was quick, hard and deeply satisfying. She sighed into his mouth and his groin tightened at the feelings it stirred.

"How about going out with me tomorrow night," he whispered close to her ear moments later when she lay curled in his arms while he held her. In the back of his mind he could still hear her cry out her response to what he'd done to her.

Dana gazed up at him. How on earth could he think of tomorrow when she was still sensually stirred up from what had happened today? She hadn't known such pure hot pleasure existed and all with the use of his fingers. She didn't want to think about what would happen if they were to actually make love. In her mind she would die a slow death, several times over.

"Tomorrow?" she said, barely getting the word out.

"Yes, tomorrow. We can go out to eat, take in a movie and then afterward walk around Stone Mountain. Anywhere that doesn't have a bed. You, lady, are too much temptation. I can only take so much."

She shifted in his arms and gazed up at him. Maybe it was her hormones talking, but when it came to Jared, she wanted to take all he had to give and not think of the consequences. "Okay, wherever you want to go is fine. I'll let you decide."

He nodded and she watched as he eased from the bed to stand. He still had his shirt and pants on and looked as rumpled as she felt. She then remembered something very important. "That was my first you know."

He glanced over at her and raised an eyebrow. "Your first what?"

She hesitated, not knowing exactly what to say or how she should say it. But as he waited for her response she knew she had to tell him of his gift to her. "My first orgasm."

He gazed at her. Shocked. When it wore off, he dropped back down on the bed and pulled her into his arms, made her look at him. "I'm glad you shared your first with me," he said huskily, meaning every word.

She smiled. "Me, too."

Jared leaned over and kissed her again, and she felt his desire but also a tenderness that overwhelmed her. He slowly pulled back, stood and crossed the room to get her shorts and T-shirt. Coming back over to the bed he took the time to redress her. He didn't say anything and neither did she.

When her clothes were back in place she looked up at him. He reached out and slid a slow finger across her cheek. "I'll call you tomorrow."

"Okay." She then remembered she needed to tell him something else. She sat up straight and pushed the hair out of her face. "I had lunch with your mom yesterday."

He startled. "You did?"

"Yes. She called and invited me to have lunch with her at Chase's Place. She's so nice, Jared, and I really hate lying to her even though I know why we're doing it."

He nodded and fixed dark eyes on her. "Don't worry about it. Things will work out."

She gave him a shaky smile. "I hope you're right." But a part of Dana wondered how things could possibly work out when the one thing that she hadn't wanted to happen was happening anyway.

She was falling in love with Jared Westmoreland.

Seven

"**W**hat do you mean there's a possibility the child is mine?" Sylvester Brewster shot to his feet.

Jared slid the documents out of the envelope and across the table as he met the man's shocked gaze. "What I'm saying is that according to this medical report, based on the physical that you took last week, you're not sterile. In fact you have a very high sperm count."

Sylvester sank back into his chair. "B-but what about that childhood disease?"

"According to Dr. Frye, you may have had a low sperm count at one time but there's no indication you were ever sterile and nothing is documented in your medical history."

Sylvester shook his head, squeezed his eyes shut. "This doesn't make sense, Jared."

"You were misinformed. Whatever doctor told your parents you were sterile evidently misdiagnosed your condition. And since you are capable of producing children, there's a strong possibility that your wife's child is yours…just like she claimed."

Sylvester dropped his head on Jared's desk with a solid thump. "Damn, Jared, you don't know what all I said to her, all the things I accused her of."

Jared nodded. He could just imagine. "All that medical report does is indicate you aren't sterile. It doesn't prove the child is definitely yours. The next step is to order an amniocentesis."

Sylvester lifted his head. "A what?"

"An amniocentesis. It's a test that's done to the mother, generally during the fourteenth to twenty-fourth week of pregnancy to determine the paternity of an unborn child. We can have the results back in two weeks."

"No."

Jared lifted a brow. "No?"

"No. I've humiliated her enough. Did you see the tabloids this morning, man? Someone leaked my accusations to the papers and it's all in the news. Jackie is never going to forgive me for not trusting her."

Jared knew that was a very strong possibility. That very morning, he had spoken to Jackie Brewster's attorney, who had informed him that his client was hurt and upset, but would be more than happy to undergo a paternity testing. Once it's proven that Sylvester *was* her baby's father, she planned to sue him for every cent he had for publicly humiliating her.

Jared met the man's stare. "I suggest you don't make decisions about anything today. Take the report home and read it and then let's meet one day next week to discuss how we're going to proceed."

"I don't want a divorce, Jared. I want my wife back. I was wrong. I should have trusted her. I love her and I owe her a huge apology."

It was on the tip of Jared's tongue to remind Sylvester that two weeks ago, when he was certain he was sterile, he'd been singing a totally different tune. "Yes, that might be the case but I doubt a reconciliation is what Mrs. Brewster has on her mind right now. According to her attorney, she doesn't want to see or talk to you. As your attorney, I suggest you don't try to contact her until we've determined our next course of action."

Thirty minutes later, Jared was standing at the window in his office looking out. Sylvester had gotten himself in a real mess this time. The love he had for his wife had gotten overshadowed with mistrust. Was there any hope of the marriage surviving? For Sylvester's sake, he hoped so.

Jared sighed deeply as he switched his thoughts from Sylvester's problems to his own. He could sum up his troubles with one name.

Dana.

There were very few times in his life when he'd been faced with a situation that he couldn't figure out or adequately handle. And this was one of those times. Frustrated and annoyed, he drew in a deep breath. What had happened between them yesterday had touched him in a way that it shouldn't have. And what was so extraordinary about it was that they hadn't made love. Yet he had shared something with her that he hadn't ever shared with another woman.

While in that bed kissing her, touching her, he had felt as if she was the only woman he could ever want. The only woman that he wanted in his lifetime. Damn, but this pretended engagement was going to his head, zapping him of common sense and confusing the hell out of him.

It hadn't been easy to leave her last night and before he'd left he had sat on the bed and pulled her into his arms. For the longest time she had sat curled up in his lap with neither of them saying anything. The only sound that had intruded on their moment had been the soft meowing of Tom at the bedroom door. Even now, just thinking about her made his chest tighten with a need he wasn't used to.

He glanced down at his watch. He would be picking her up at six for dinner. And the only thing he could think about was seeing her again and kissing her with the desperation he felt. Dana Rollins was definitely getting under his skin.

"Would you like some more wine?"

"No, thank you, Jared." Dana bit down softly on her lip and tried not to stare at him. Every time their gazes met she felt a tiny pull at her heart.

"Are you ready for your trip this weekend?"

She met his gaze and forced a smile. "Yes, I'm ready. Since it's not a long trip, a lot of packing isn't necessary."

"I'd like to go with you."

Dana's eyes widened in surprise. "Why?"

Jared shrugged as he sank back in his chair. That was a good question since he had just made the decision. "I don't like the idea of you driving so many hours alone."

Dana couldn't help but appreciate his concerns. "It's something I do every year, Jared. And when my father's birthday comes around in September I'll be doing it again. No big deal."

Jared frowned. To him it was a big deal. "You shared my father's birthday with me and I want to be there to share your mother's birthday with you."

Dana glanced down at her wineglass. How could she not fall in love with him when he said something like that? She slowly lifted her head and met his gaze. "Thanks, Jared, but that's not necessary."

He smiled. "It is to me." He leaned closer over the table. "Besides, it's been years since I've been to Jekyll Island and I'd like to go there again."

Dana inhaled deeply. The part of her that was fighting what she was feeling for Jared wanted to tell him to find another time to go, that she needed time alone, time away from him, but she couldn't say that. She decided to use another approach. "I don't think it's a good idea for us to go out of town together, Jared."

"Why? Because of last night?"

Dana felt a jolt to her body at the memories, something she'd tried to downplay all day. She had played Red Light, Green Light, many times as a child but never like that and never with a playmate like Jared. He gave the game a whole new meaning. "That, among other things," she finally said softly. *And please don't ask me what those other things are,* she silently screamed. *I don't want you to know that I'm falling in love with you.*

"I know your thoughts on us sleeping together, Dana. You've been pretty clear on that and I think I've been straightforward in saying that I won't push you into doing anything you're not ready for. But this isn't about us sharing a bed."

Dana met his gaze. "Then what's it about, Jared?"

His eyes held hers. "It's about me being with you and enjoying your company. I like talking to you."

Dana knew he was holding something back. She had been around him enough to know when something was bothering him. She could feel it. "Is there something else? Is everything all right with your mother, Jared?"

He stared at her for a moment and after taking a deep breath he said, "I spoke with Dad earlier today and he said that Mom got a call from the hospital. There was a cancellation and they were able to schedule her outpatient surgery for next week instead of waiting two weeks."

Dana nodded. "That's good news, isn't it?"

Jared heaved a long sigh. "Yes, but…"

She waited for him to finish. When he hesitated she asked, "But what?"

He dragged a hand over the back of his neck, seemingly frustrated. "But nothing. I guess I'm just remembering how it was the last time."

Dana understood and reached out, took his hand in hers and held it tight. A part of her was glad she was here with him and that he was sharing his innermost fears with her. "All we can do is hope and pray for the best, Jared. And I know you, your father and your brothers appreciate and love your mother. Your willingness to pretend to be engaged just to make her happy proves how much you care."

Dana let go of his hand and sat back, hoping she'd

said something to make him feel better. She could tell he was worried but a part of her believed Sarah Westmoreland would come through this just fine.

"How did your parents meet?" she decided to ask, wanting him to dwell on happier memories.

She watched the corners of his lips turn up into a smile. "My mother and Aunt Evelyn were best friends growing up in Birmingham, Alabama. When they graduated from high school, Aunt Evelyn came to Atlanta to visit her aunt. During her first week here she went on a church outing and met Uncle John. She wrote back to my mom telling her she had fallen in love and asking her to come to Atlanta to be her maid of honor. She'd only known her new groom a little more than a week!"

Jared gave her a lopsided grin. "My mother, being the levelheaded person that she is, caught a bus that same day and arrived in town to talk some sense into Aunt Evelyn. She didn't think love at first sight was possible."

Dana chuckled. She could just imagine his mother doing that. "What happened next?"

Jared smiled. "She got to town, met John's twin brother, James, and fell for him just as hard as Aunt Evelyn had fallen for my uncle. My parents got married within a couple of weeks of my aunt and uncle's wedding."

A smile softened Dana's lips. "That's a beautiful love story."

Jared shrugged as he took a sip of his drink. "Yes, it is, isn't it?" It had been a long time since he had thought about how his parents had gotten together. They had met and fallen in love immediately. They hadn't thought about any of the ups and downs they would face. They had simply loved each other and had wanted to be together. To them that was all that had mattered.

Sighing deeply, Jared glanced down at his watch. "Are you ready to leave? Tonight is a nice night to walk around the park. Would you like to do that?"

"I'd love to." Dana met his gaze, suddenly understanding his need to get away for a few days and making a quick decision. "I'd love your company this weekend if you're serious about going with me to Brunswick."

He smiled warmly. "I am."

She returned his smile. "Good."

Over an hour later Jared returned to Dana's home and walked her to the door. She turned and looked at him.

"I enjoyed being with you tonight, Dana," he said, taking her hands in his.

Jared's words, spoken in a soft husky voice, immediately reclaimed Dana's attention. And his touch sent all kinds of sensations escalating through her body. "I enjoyed being with you tonight, as well," she said honestly. "Would you like to come in for something to drink?"

He shook his head. "No, it's late and I'd better go."

Dana let out the breath she'd been holding. A part of her was glad he had turned down her invitation but then another part was disappointed. She wanted to be alone with him. She wanted him to kiss her again. And more.

She gazed up at him. "Then I guess we need to say good night."

He gently tugged on her hand, pulling her from the shaft of light shining down on them from the porch light to a darkened area of the porch. She saw the kiss coming, wanted it and moaned with pleasure the moment their mouths touched. Intense heat, overwhelming pleasure shot through her as his tongue masterfully mated with hers. She could only stand there and grip his solid shoulders for support as he took her to another world, feasting on her lips as if they were a meal he had to savor.

When he finally released her mouth she had to rest her head on his chest while she caught her breath. Jared Westmoreland could incite passion with a mere touch, a kiss, a look. And she had felt his solid hard erection pressing against her, through the material of her skirt. He was as aroused and as she was.

"Go into the house, Dana," he whispered against her lips after slowly releasing her. He took a step back.

She swallowed. His voice sounded hoarse, husky, and sexy. "Good night, Jared," she said and turned to unlock the door.

"Good night. I'm playing pool with my cousins and Reggie tomorrow night, but I'll be by early Saturday to pick you up. Is seven o'clock a good time?"

She turned to him and wished she hadn't. He had stepped back into the light and stood tall and looked handsome. His coat jacket was slung over his shoulder and held in place by his fingertips. The pose was unforgettably sexy.

She cleared her throat. "Yes, seven will be fine. I'll be packed and ready to go."

"All right."

Giving him one last look, Dana opened the door and slipped inside. She leaned against the closed door when she heard him walk away, and then moments later the sound of his car leaving.

It was only then that she was able to slow down the beating of her heart and breathe easy again. How would she ever survive a weekend alone with Jared Westmoreland?

Jared stood next to Dana and watched as she placed the bouquet of fresh flowers on her mother's grave.

When he had picked her up bright and early she had been friendly and perky, the complete opposite of him first thing in the morning. He could be a bear until he downed at least two cups of coffee. But she had opened the door all smiles, packed and ready to go.

During the drive they had talked about a number of things including early memories of the time she'd spent in Brunswick, backyard cookouts with her parents, going to church together as a family on Sundays and how she would greet her father at the door whenever he'd come home from work.

They stopped once for lunch, but otherwise they had driven straight to town. Once there they had found a florist shop to purchase the flowers and had then driven to the cemetery.

He had considered remaining in the car, letting her have her private moments, but a part of him wanted to be with her, to stand beside her and let her know that he was there and that he cared. After a few moments of silence she straightened and automatically, as if it was the most natural thing to do, she leaned up against him and he offered her the support she needed.

He wrapped his arms around her shoulders and held her close to him. "You okay?" he asked softly.

She tried to smile and the effort made Jared's throat tighten when he saw the tears in her eyes. "Yes, I'm fine. It's just harder this year more than ever because today would have been their thirtieth wedding anniversary. They got married on my mother's birthday."

Dana gazed up at him through misty eyes. "Mom always reminded Dad that she should get two gifts that day instead of one, and of course he always came through. They loved each other very much, Jared. In a way I think if they had to die it was better for them to go together. I can't imagine my father living a normal life without my mother or vice versa. They had dated since high school and were so close, so connected. But the beauty of it all was that they never made me feel like I was an outsider. Dad used to say that I was the greatest gift of their love."

Jared nodded, knowing she needed to talk, get her feelings and emotions out. He was jarred into the realization that some marriages endured. Her parents' had. So had his parents' and his aunt and uncle's marriage. For a long moment they didn't say anything, they just stood there, needing the silence. He admired her ability to do this, to come here twice a year and face the pain of her loss with the poise and grace he had come to associate with her. He couldn't imagine getting a call, saying that both his parents were gone—unexpectedly, just like that. And if that were to happen, at least he had his brothers, the entire Westmoreland family. Dana had no one.

But today she had him and he wanted her to know that. He reached for her hand, linking their fingers. He was glad he had come, pleased that he was with her in this place, sharing such a personal and private moment. It meant a lot to him that it was his shoulder she was leaning on, his hand she was holding. And for the very first time in his life he felt he was in danger.

Danger of losing his heart.

"Thanks, Jared."

He tipped his head and looked at her. "You don't have to thank me, Dana. At the moment, I can't think of any place I'd rather be than here with you." And he meant it. "Ready to go?"

"Yes, I'm ready."

Back in the car, Jared headed toward Jekyll Island. His secretary had made hotel reservations for them. If Jeannie had thought it odd that he'd told her to get two separate rooms she hadn't said anything.

He glanced over at Dana. "Are you hungry?"

She shook her head. "No, in fact I think I'm beat and going to take a nap when we get to the hotel and check in."

He smiled. She might feel tired, but she didn't look it. She looked great dressed in a pair of slacks and top. He spared her another quick glance. There hadn't been one time he'd seen her that he hadn't gotten turned on by what she was wearing.

Jared could see them in one bed, in each other's arms doing a number of things, and taking a nap wasn't one of them.

Dana woke up from her dream with a start, her breathing uneven, a wave of heat slowly building and touching her in her most intimate places. She closed her eyes to recapture the moments when she had imagined

Jared in bed with her, naked with his arms around her, holding her, and his aroused body pressed intimately against her pelvis, sending her over the edge as he tried to connect with her.

She had felt the dampness of his skin, the perfection of his muscles as they clenched beneath her palms and the texture of his chest hair rubbing against her breasts, hardening the tips.

She had experienced all those things. But only in her dream.

Dana pulled herself up in bed and inhaled deeply as she pushed her hair from her face. She'd known she was a goner when he had walked her to her hotel-room door. After saying that he hoped she enjoyed her nap, he had lifted her palm to his lips and placed a kiss at her wrist. And it hadn't been your typical wrist kissing. His hot, wet tongue had slid over her wrist and then he had gently sucked the area, leaving a mark. His mark.

She glanced down at her wrist. She still felt the heat. She then looked across the room at the closed door that separated his room from hers—a shield, a barrier, a connecting door. But if it were to open…

She wondered if he was there. Had he taken a nap, as well? Had he dreamed of her as she had dreamed of him?

Slipping out of bed she stood and decided it was time to take part in some sort of physical pleasure. The other night Jared had shown her just what her body had been missing. He had given her a taste of what pleasures were out there if she decided to indulge.

Visiting her parents' graves had made her realize just how unpredictable life could be. You could be here today and gone tomorrow. Life held no guarantees, there were no promises. There were no forevers.

There was only the moment. And you had to seize it to get what you wanted, capture it, slow it down and take advantage of it, make every second count.

Jared had always been honest with her, totally up-front. She knew how he felt about serious involvements. And she knew that no matter what, he had no intentions of changing his mind about that. Next week, if things worked out with his mother, he would walk away, just as surely as there was a sun shining in the sky. But dammit, she refused to let go without at least having something to look back on and remember from their time together.

She turned when she heard the gentle knock on the connecting door. Tightening the belt of her silk robe, she crossed the room and slowly opened it. Jared was there. She inhaled gently, breathing in the manly scent of him. He stood tall, handsome, hot and sexy. His features were sharp; the eyes that were holding hers were keen. She felt her heart beat violently at such profound sexiness.

Regardless of whether Jared was dressed as a million-dollar businessman or wearing faded jeans and a chambray shirt, as he was now, he looked like a man any woman would want both in and out of her bed. The man any woman would want to strip her naked, kiss her senseless and make love to her with an all-consuming passion.

And the man a woman would want to give her heart to on a silver platter.

Suddenly, she knew she was no longer falling in love with him. She *had* fallen in love with him. She loved him with every sense of her being, with every ounce of blood flowing fast and furious through her veins, with the breaths she was now taking—slow and uneven. Over the past couple of weeks she had seen more than a glimpse of him. She had gotten to know him as a man of high intelligence and intense integrity. He had proven it that day when she had shown up at his office, spitting fire and mad as hell. Luther had been his client, yet he had gone beyond what some would consider ethically proper and had given her off-the-record advice to save herself from further embarrassment, humiliation and financial ruin. And for that she truly appreciated him.

She also appreciated the way he showed her that sex wasn't overrated, and that with the right person it could be a definitely satisfying and gratifying experience. And even now, here, today, he had come to Brunswick with her. He had stood beside her and had given her his shoulder to lean on when the pain of losing her parents had resurfaced.

"I hope I didn't wake you from your nap, Dana."

She swallowed deeply as she stared up at him. "No, I'm awake." *In more ways than one,* she thought. "Did you sleep?"

He smiled, and his smile sent sensations oozing through the pit of her stomach. "No, I found that I couldn't sleep after all and decided to catch a tennis match on television."

He glanced beyond her and she knew his eyes lit on her rumpled bed. He returned his gaze to her. "Do you find the accommodations acceptable?" he asked softly.

Dana couldn't stop the smile that touched her lips. The accommodations were more than acceptable. He had made reservations at one of the most expensive hotels on the beach, right on the ocean, connecting suites with balconies facing the water. She had offered to share the cost but he refused to talk about it. "Everything is wonderful, Jared. Thank you. I hadn't expected such extravagance."

Jared nodded. He knew she hadn't and that was one of the things that made her so special and unique. Because of his success other women had expected certain luxuries. Dana expected nothing but in his opinion she deserved everything.

He considered how sexy she looked now, wearing a leopard-print robe that was destined to bring out the beast in any man. It hadn't helped matters when he had glanced over and saw her bed with the messed-up covers and tangled sheets.

"Would you like to take a walk on the beach before dinner?" he decided to ask. "We can either eat in the restaurant downstairs or, if you prefer, we can dine in our rooms."

Dana lowered her gaze and quickly made her decision—about a number of things. She tipped her chin up and met his gaze. "I'd love to take a walk on the beach and if you don't mind I'd prefer if we ate here."

"All right."

She continued to hold his gaze and in the dark depths of his eyes she knew that he recognized that something had changed. Something elemental and deep. She also knew he would keep his word. He would take things slow, be patient and let her take the lead. He wouldn't push, he wouldn't pressure, but he would be ready whenever she was. And when he pounced, there would be no stopping him. God, she hoped not. She wanted it all. Everything he had to give. And she knew when it happened there was no going back. Their time together was limited. The moments would be short. But she intended to make the most of them, and when he walked away, she would have special memories to last a lifetime.

"I guess I'd better let you get dressed then," he said, breaking into her thoughts.

She smiled at him. "Yes, I think you'd better if we want to take that walk while there's still a lot of daylight."

He nodded. Then slowly he leaned down and captured her lips. It was a slow, drugging kiss, gentle, tender. Whether he was kissing her this way or devouring her mouth, it didn't matter. He still knew how to rob her of her senses and want to make her scream out for more.

He slowly released her lips but kept his attention glued to them as she took her tongue and licked her mouth. She heard his sharp intake of breath, saw his guts clench and knew he was walking the same tightrope that she was.

"I'll knock on the door when I'm ready," she whispered, and when he nodded and took a step back, she gently closed the door and leaned against it. Throwing an arm over her eyes she inhaled deeply. What a kiss! Her already hot body had gone up another degree. The man was a master at seduction but she wouldn't have him any other way.

A smile touched her just-kissed lips. Jared was an excellent teacher. And although she knew there were more lessons to be learned, he had given her enough tutoring for what she needed to do.

At that moment the only thing she could think of was her plans to take on Jared Westmoreland.

Eight

If Jared didn't know any better he would swear Dana was trying to drive him mad. Mad with desire.

He doubted very seriously if he could hold on to his sanity, as well as his control, much longer. At any moment he would snap and Dana would drive him to reach across the table, snatch her into his arms and have her for dessert. *Dana Delight* would definitely be a mouth-watering temptation, a delectable treat.

The seduction started when she had knocked on the connecting door to let him know she was ready to go walking on the beach. He had been literally blown away by her outfit, a pair of denim shorts and a white halter top. He had seen halter tops before but never this enticing. He'd been tempted to untie the damn thing and set her breasts free. And he didn't want to think about how sensual her flat stomach looked totally bare, showing off the navel he'd grown so fond of a few days ago.

They had held hands while walking along the beach, enjoying the sunset and the ocean. They had talked about a lot of things. The weather, the economy, books they had read and exotic foods they had eaten. The conversation then shifted to the Westmoreland family and how they looked forward to the birth of Storm and Jayla's twins in a few months. Dana listened, hearing the excitement in Jared's voice. She felt a tinge of sadness that she wouldn't be around to share in the excitement since she would be out of the picture by then, out of Jared's life. At some point, he must have realized it, too. She glanced up, saw him staring at her and the intensity in his gaze gave her pause. The twins were a stark reminder that the two of them didn't have a future together. During the remainder of their walk, conversation ceased. They were caught up in their own private thoughts—thoughts they preferred not to share with each other.

When they returned to the hotel, they reluctantly went their separate ways to dress for dinner and within an hour's time, the food had been wheeled into Jared's suite. Even he would admit it was a night of romance with the candles burning on the table and the soft music playing in the background, compliments of the hotel's management. Evidently Jeannie had mentioned when she'd made reservations that they were a recently engaged couple and the hotel staff wanted to be remembered, in case they were undecided as to where they would spend their honeymoon.

A honeymoon that would never take place.

For the second time that day, Jared felt numb, his

feelings paralyzed. All he could think about was that he and Dana didn't have a future together. He forced himself to get a grip and refused to dwell on that now. All he wanted to think about was the woman sitting across from him, who was slowly sipping her champagne—another compliment of the hotel—as she watched him through beautiful dark eyes.

His body's temperature rose a few degrees. All during dinner he had been turned on by everything she did. Even watching as she opened her mouth to eat her food had stirred a flame of arousal within him. She had a pair of sensuous lips and every time she used them he felt his loins burning.

He couldn't help but wonder what she was thinking. She hadn't been talkative and the attorney in him, the one whose senses were sharp and mind alert, was waiting patiently for her to say something. Anything that would give him an indication of what was going on inside her head.

Since the suspense was killing him, he decided to just ask. "A penny for your thoughts."

Dana placed her glass down on the table. An intimate smile played at the edges of her mouth. "I was just thinking about you and how grateful I am that you came and how much I enjoy your company."

"I enjoy yours, as well."

And he really meant it. He had dined with other women but this was the first time he had felt so totally comfortable. So at ease with a beautiful woman that he both liked and desired.

"You mentioned earlier that you wanted to talk to me about a party that Thorn and Tara are giving," Dana said, recapturing his attention.

He fixed his gaze on her, looking fully into her eyes. "The weekend after Mother's Day is Thorn and Tara's first wedding anniversary. They're planning a huge celebration and I wanted to make sure you're free to attend with me that Friday night."

Dana's smile faltered. "But that's two weeks after your mother's surgery."

Jared nodded. "Yes. Is there a problem with that?"

She thought there was. "I assumed that if things were fine with your mother's surgery that we wouldn't..."

When it became apparent that she was having difficulty completing her statement, Jared reached across the table and took her hand in his. "That we wouldn't what?" he asked softly.

"Be seeing each other again, that you'd end things, break our engagement."

Jared stared into dark brown questioning eyes as he thought for a moment. Although he understood what she was saying and agreed that at one time he had thought breaking up with her as soon as possible was best for all concerned, there were a few things he felt they should take into account.

"My family, especially my mother, will find it rather odd that we broke our engagement so soon after her surgery. I think we should at least wait a couple of weeks before dropping the bomb on them." *And I don't know how I'll let you go.*

Dana couldn't see putting off the inevitable. "We're going to have to end things sooner or later, Jared. We can't continue to deceive everyone."

Jared stared at the hand he was holding then slowly released it. "I guess you're right. If things work out and my mother won't need any further treatments, then maybe the night of Thorn and Tara's party should be the last time we see each other. Agreed?"

Dana tipped up her chin and held his gaze. "Yes. Agreed." She knew that meant they had only three weeks left to spend together. Already she felt a deep pain in her heart but refused to let it ruin her evening.

"Dinner was wonderful," she said dabbing at her mouth with a napkin.

Heat flared within Jared. He would have been more than willing to wipe away any lingering crumbs from around her lips with his tongue.

He reached up and loosened the top button of his shirt. For dinner he had dressed casually, wearing a pair of khaki slacks and a black collared shirt. Dana was wearing a beautiful printed dress that had an endless slit up the side. That dress had nearly driven him crazy before she had finally taken a seat for dinner.

Moments later, his gut clenched. It seemed she was about to drive him crazy all over again. "I like the view from the balcony," she said, taking her glass and walking over to the double French doors.

"Yes. Gorgeous." He liked the view, as well, but he wasn't talking about what was on the other side of those French doors. The view he was feasting his eyes on was right in this very room.

"I bet it's simply beautiful at night," she said softly, turning around and meeting his gaze, looking at him with something akin to desire in her eyes. He shook his head wondering if that's what he actually saw or what he wanted to see.

"I bet it is, too," he managed to say as his gaze did a

long, slow slide down the length of her body. "If you stick around for a while, I'm sure we'll see just how beautiful it is. It won't be long before it's completely dark."

A smile creased the corners of her eyes. "Can you imagine standing out there under those stars?"

It was on the tip of his tongue to say he would rather be lying down under those stars and making love to her. He picked up his own glass and slowly walked over to her. When he came to a stop in front of her, a thick silence hung over them as he held her gaze, watched her uneven breathing and smelled her scent.

Aroused.

He was an experienced man. A man who knew women. And he would recognize that scent anywhere, especially with Dana. It was the same scent he'd drowned in that night they played Red Light, Green Light. The same one that had almost driven him over the edge while watching her first orgasm. If there was any way he could bottle that scent he would. Tonight it mingled with the fragrance of the seductive perfume she was wearing and the combination was a very passion-stirring force.

"Let's make a toast."

Her words broke the silence and his deep concentration. "And what would you like us to toast, Dana?" he asked huskily. Intense desire was mounting within him. It wouldn't take much for him to drop to his knees, lift her dress and go straight to the source of that scent. Both his fingers and his tongue itched to—

"I propose that we toast life."

He met her gaze as his mind was jerked back to attention. "Life?"

"Yes. It can be taken from you in a second, a minute, at any place, anytime. That's why you should live life to the fullest. Enjoy it. Appreciate it. Because when it's gone, it's over. And there's nothing you can do about it."

Jared considered her words. *Life.* He couldn't help but think of how different his had been since she had walked into it. Stormed into it was a better word. In a span of less than eight weeks, he had met her, introduced her to his family and given them the definite impression they were engaged, had purchased a very costly ring for her—one he intended for her to keep—and had spent the last couple of weeks pretending to be a man very much in love. To say that Dana Rollins hadn't affected his life would be an understatement.

"Okay, we'll toast to life," he said, lifting his glass to connect with hers. They took a sip of their champagne.

"Umm, want to have some fun?" she asked, holding his gaze over the rim of her glass.

Jared lifted a brow. "What kind of fun?"

A smile turned up her lips. "I'd like to play a game," she said softly.

"A game?"

"Yes. A game of hide-and-seek. I hide, you find me."

Jared smiled. He liked the thought of doing that. "And what happens when I find you?"

She returned his smile. "That depends."

"On what?"

"Where I'm found."

Jared downplayed the possibilities as he glanced around the room. "There aren't many places you can hide."

She grinned. "Oh, between my room and yours I'm sure there's a few."

Jared was tempted to tell her that hiding from him wouldn't do any good since her scent would give her away. When it came to her, his nose was like radar.

"All right. So what do you want me to do?" he asked, more than willing to play this game she'd suggested.

"Leave the room for about ten minutes. When you come back, the suite will be totally dark, and remember I'll be either hiding in my suite or yours."

Jared nodded. This was the second game they had played together, and for someone who usually lived a structured life, he was enjoying letting go and being adventurous with Dana.

He began walking toward the door. "Ten minutes. That's all I'm giving you. Then I'll be back, whether you're ready or not."

Dana watched as he gave her one last stomach-churning smile before opening the door, walking out of it and closing it behind him. She slowly crossed the room and dropped down on the floral-printed sofa and kicked off her sandals. She inhaled deeply and smiled seductively.

She would definitely be ready when he returned.

Jared returned ten minutes later. Ten minutes on the nose and not one second more.

He opened his door and stepped into the darkened room. He couldn't help but be amused as he switched on a light. Dana must have figured her scent would give her away so she had liberally sprayed his suite with the perfume she'd been wearing.

He glanced around the room and noticed her sandals

were by his sofa. Evidently she had kicked them off there. He walked over and picked one up. They were pretty and boy did she have small feet, sexy feet. He placed the shoe back down and glanced at the sofa. It seemed her shoes weren't the only thing she had left behind. He picked up the scarf she'd worn around her waist.

He glanced around, his ears on alert. The door connecting their suites was open. He crossed the room to go into hers. It was dark and he turned on a lamp. His gaze looked around, nothing looked amiss, and there wasn't a sound to be heard. And the scent of her perfume was in this room, as well. He walked out of the bedroom to the sitting area. He looked down in front of the sofa and blinked. There in a pool on the floor was her dress.

His breath caught exactly the same moment his arousal thickened. This was definitely one hell of a game she was playing. He hadn't expected it to take this turn so quickly, but he wasn't complaining. He had told her that he would leave it up to her to let him know if and when she was ready to take their relationship to another level. This was her way of letting him know she was ready.

Now it was his job to find her.

He was the hunter and would find his prey. With a determined purpose he walked across the room to the small kitchen that had a breakfast bar and table. He opened a closet door and found it empty.

He then retraced his steps back to her bedroom and went to check out her bathroom. He found it almost empty. A red lace bra was hanging from a light in the ceiling. He reached up and pulled it down.

He was getting hot.

Walking back to her room he got on his knees and looked under the huge king-size bed and found nothing. He looked in the closet and came up empty. He opened the French doors and walked out on the balcony. It was bare.

Frustration, added to intense arousal, wasn't a good thing. The pressure of his erection against his pants was almost killing him. When he found Dana she would pay dearly for this torture. He walked back through the connecting door into his suite and glanced around. The bedroom door was closed and he distinctly remembered it being open when he'd left.

An enticing possibility flooded his mind, made his body harden even more as he slowly crossed the room. He glanced down the moment he reached for the doorknob and saw red lace. Leaning down he picked it up. It wasn't much, barely a scrap, but he definitely knew what it was and where it came from.

Bringing the item to his nose he inhaled Dana's scent, a different one than the perfume. It was a womanly scent that was all hers. Privately. Exclusively. Deciding that she definitely wouldn't need it anymore tonight, he slipped her thong into his back pocket. Slowly opening the bedroom door, he walked into darkness and closed the door behind him.

Dana held her breath. Jared had finally found her. Not that she had done a good job at hiding. She thought she had made it easy for him but evidently she hadn't.

She had known the exact moment he had returned and had heard every step he'd taken around the room.

She'd known when he had searched her suite and when he had returned to his own. And now he was here, in his bedroom, and she was in his bed, totally naked and waiting for him.

Her mind was made up, her decision final, with no regrets. When he walked away she would have reminders of this night. They would be memories that would last her a lifetime because she knew whatever he did, Jared never did anything halfway. He was meticulously thorough and methodically efficient.

"I know you're in here, Dana," he whispered huskily in the darkened room. "And ready or not, here I come."

She heard his footsteps, slow, yet determined. She heard the sound of his breathing, quick and uneven. She almost held her breath when he came closer and closer to the bed. She felt his presence and smelled his masculine scent.

And when he switched on the lamp, bathing the room with a soft translucent glow, their gazes connected. Held. Then slowly, his gaze drifted from her face and moved downward to the sheet that covered her nude body. Then it moved back up to her face. It was a while before he spoke.

"I found you," he said in a raspy voice that was so husky it stirred heat all over her skin. "So what do I get?"

She paused a moment before saying, "Anything you want."

A hint of a smile touched his lips. Intense desire darkened his eyes. "Anything?"

"Yes, *anything*."

He continued to hold her gaze. "Are you sure?" he asked moments later.

"Positive."

His sensuous smile deepened. "And you're ready?" he asked, wanting to be doubly sure that she was. Once he began making love to her, he would be hard-pressed to stop. Unable to help himself he reached out and pushed away a strand of hair that had fallen in her face. He needed to touch her, connect with her on any level.

"Yes, I'm ready."

"With no regrets?"

She inhaled slowly. Knowing what he was asking and why. Nothing had changed. Sooner or later, possibly even sooner, depending on the results of his mother's surgery, he would be walking out of her life. She knew it. Had accepted it. And would be prepared when it happened.

But she wanted to seize the moment. Celebrate life. With him. "There won't be any regrets, Jared. I knew the score going into this game."

She then slowly eased up, letting the sheet fall away, hearing his sharp intake of breath when it did so. Getting on her knees she brushed her hand against his chest and moved slowly downward to feel the hard planes of his stomach. "Are we going to talk all night or are we going to get on with what we've wanted for quite a while?"

He reached out and traced a path around her nipple with his finger, teasing the darkened tip. "And what is it that you think we've wanted?"

"Some of each other."

"Some?"

Her lips smiled with warm confidence. "Okay, I stand corrected. *All* of each other."

Without giving her the chance to draw her next

breath, Jared pulled her into his arms and covered her mouth with his, igniting an explosion of passion between them. He kissed her with hungry intensity. It seemed as if a dam had burst, emotions were flooding and there was no one around to fix it.

Dana's arms came around him and held on, taking everything he had to give and wondering how she had denied herself for so long. Jared was a special man who had always treated her like a lady. And for that she would always be eternally grateful.

He slowly released her and stepped back. Her legs trembled from the impact of his kiss. He continued to hold her gaze, looking at her with virile intensity, as he unbuckled his belt. She felt heat pouring into her stomach and drifting downward between her legs as she began catching fire from his flame.

"Tonight I'm going to do all those things I've been dreaming of doing to you," Jared said, his voice a thin whisper and full of sexual need. "I want to see you reach a climax again, several of them, over and over. But this time, you won't be alone. I'll be there with you, joining in and sharing the pleasure." His words were seduction all wrapped in silk.

Dana watched as he pulled his shirt over his head. With the top of him bare, he exuded strength, power and muscular endurance. He had a beautiful chest and his dark coloring made him look even more beautiful to her. He tossed the shirt aside, then sat down in a wing chair to remove his shoes and socks. After that was done, he stood and went back to his pants, tugging the belt from the loops.

He smiled over at her. "When I told you that I

wouldn't push until you were ready, I knew that meant my patience would be tested. I've been wanting you forever and tonight I plan to show you just how much."

Dana continued to watch as he slid down his pants and underwear. She blinked when she saw the size of him. She had felt his hardened erection plenty of times against her but now seeing it in the flesh was putting a whole new spin on things. Jared was loaded. He had been very fortunate when certain body parts had been distributed.

"Umm, interesting," she whispered softly, meeting his gaze and smiling.

He chuckled. "Interesting? Is that all you can say?"

"I'll wait to make sure it can work before making any more comments."

He laughed, loving every moment of sharing this camaraderie with her, while at the same time fire bolts of desire raced through him. "Trust me. It will work. In fact I plan for it to go into overtime."

The room got quiet as the reality of what they were about to do set in. For the longest time, their gazes connected and their minds were of one accord. Naked, Jared slowly walked over to the bed and took Dana's hands in his. He brought them to his lips and kissed her palms.

"You do things to me that no other woman ever has, Dana. You make me feel things. Make me want things. I don't want you to think what we're about to do is just another roll between the sheets for me. It's something I consider exceptional and extraordinary."

The love Dana felt for Jared increased tenfold. She loved him with all her heart. Tonight she wanted to physically connect with the man she loved. Deciding he had talked enough, she tugged on his hands and they tumbled down into the bed.

Jared's body ended up on top of hers and he glanced down at her, feeling the heat of flesh touching flesh, and framed her face with his palms. He studied her features as if implanting them in his memory.

And then he kissed her. Hungrily. Devouringly. And he couldn't stop. He wanted her with a vengeance, a deep-rooted passion that he couldn't understand. He heard the gentle moan of passion that escaped her lips, and felt the warmth of her fingers caress his naked skin as his tongue continued to ravage the sweetness of her mouth. Finally, the need to breathe and to shield her from pregnancy made him pull away. "I have to protect you," he said with hot desire running rampant in his voice.

He slowly stood, crossed back over the room for his pants. He fished through his pocket, pulling out her underwear instead of his wallet. He glanced over at her and smiled. "Nice color."

She gave him a short laugh brushed with embarrassment. "Glad you like it."

Tossing them aside he then checked his other pocket for his wallet, pulled it out and retrieved a condom packet. Several. He knew she was watching as he put it on, and was overwhelmed by the sensations that rammed through him as he prepared to bury himself in her softness.

After he finished the task he glanced up and met her gaze. "What do you think?"

He saw the heated desire in her eyes, saw the slight

shivering of her body. "I think," she said softly, "that more than anything, I want you inside of me, Jared."

Jared inhaled sharply as he felt a tightening coil in his lower region. He should have known she would say or do something to endear her to him that much more. He wanted to fight it but couldn't. And he knew what he was feeling had nothing to do with the length of time it had been since he'd had a woman. It had everything to do with this particular woman.

He slowly walked over to the bed, slid in and pulled her into his arms. Emotions he'd never felt before took their toll and he kissed her while giving in to his overheated senses. He then moved from her lips to her breasts, determined to top what he'd done to them the other day. The lips and tongue torturing her now were those of a man who wanted to make his woman as wet as she could get. Torture was too mild a word to use for what he was doing. He took his time reacquainting himself with the taste of her skin, the feel of her flesh, liking the way her nipples hardened in his mouth as he feasted on them greedily.

When her scent became intoxicating and way too potent, his hand moved in slow precision and reached downward to touch the most intimate part of her, finding her not just wet but completely drenched. He vividly remembered a scene from one of his dreams that he longed to act out. He shifted his body and moved away from her breasts, began tracing a path down her chest to her navel with his mouth, glorying in the sensual taste of her naked skin.

He continued to trail kisses all over her. Rolling her on her stomach, placed kisses all over her spine, the center of her back and all over her shoulders. He then gently rolled her back over and met her gaze. By the look in her eyes he knew she was trying to contemplate his next move. He leaned back and without saying a word, his hand traveled between her legs, parting them just seconds before he lowered his mouth to her with hungry intensity.

Of their own accord, her hips lifted to him and to make sure they stayed there, he grabbed hold of them, held them as he greedily devoured her in this very intimate way. He heard her moan with every insistent stroke of his tongue. He tasted her heat, her fire and her passion. Passion he was both creating and satisfying.

"Jared!"

He quickly pulled back and covered her body with his, interlocking their limbs. He took her mouth at the same time he entered her, sliding inside of her in one smooth thrust as she welcomed him into her body. The same heat consuming her was eating him alive. He began moving as sensations, too overpowering to be real, clamored through him, making his strokes harder, stronger and deeper, robbing him of any logical thought but one. *Don't hold back. Share everything with her and deal with the consequences later.*

And when her body exploded into what seemed like a billion pieces beneath him and carried her to a spiraling climax, he broke their kiss and buried his face in her neck. Kissed her there. Marked her. He continued to take her over the edge with steady thrusts of possession.

That same explosion, the finality of every physical sensation he could think of, overtook him. He hollered out her name as his body shook with the magnitude of an earthquake, the force of a hurricane and the electrifying power of a thunderstorm. What he had found in her arms, inside her body was intense pleasure, too magnificent to measure and too rapturous to describe.

And he knew as the earth slowly ceased spinning and his body relaxed, utterly consumed and feeling like a lifeless weight floating on shafts of air, that this was an experience he'd never shared with any woman before. He was bombarded with the need to hold her and make love to her all through the night.

At that very moment, Jared had to concede that when the time came, walking away from her would be the hardest thing he'd ever had to do.

Shortly after midnight, Jared stood barefoot on the balcony and leaned against the railing. The incessant pounding of the waves beating against the shore matched the raggedness of his breathing and the distinctive hammering of his heart.

Emotions that he had never dealt with before were coming at him from all directions, different angles, crowding in on him. He released a long deep breath as he tried to fight them. But it was useless. Dana had touched him tonight in a way no other woman had, and it hadn't been all physical.

It seemed that after making love to her that first time, an undeniable urge to do so again and again had taken over, and so they had all through the night. He had shared more than just his body with her. He had also shared his soul. It seemed as if she had somehow eased inside his heart and was still snuggled there.

After making love to her the last time he had lain

awake while she drifted off to sleep beside him. Sighs of satisfaction had continued to flow through his body long afterward. When he'd glanced over at her, he had been touched by how peaceful she looked. Struggling with feelings that were foreign to him, he had slid out of bed and slipped into his pants. Before he had left the room he had glanced back, lingering in the doorway. The moonlight shining in through the window focused on Dana curled in his bed, her naked body barely covered while she slept. Her bare breasts, firm and full, had tempted him to taste them again.

Bringing his thoughts back to the present, Jared pulled in a broken breath, knowing that no matter how many women he'd slept with before Dana and no matter how many he would sleep with after, he would only find total, complete and satisfying release in her arms. Only hers.

Jared turned slowly, sensing Dana's presence immediately. A lump thickened in his throat when he saw she was wearing his shirt, a shirt that barely covered her.

Their eyes met. Held. And then she said softly, "I woke up and decided that it was lonely in bed without you."

Jared didn't want to tell her the reason he'd left was that he had needed distance from her; he'd been driven to have a few moments alone to get his head back on straight. Making love to her had literally blown him away. Instead he told her part of the truth. "I wanted to hear the sound of the ocean and see the moon and all the stars."

He drew in a deep breath of air, not able to think beyond the need she aroused in him, and then added slowly. "But do you know what I want now more than anything?"

Dana shook her head. "No. What?"

"To make love to you again." A part of him wished he could have mustered enough strength to have said that for the remainder of the night they needed to sleep in separate beds; they were getting into something neither had counted on, something he definitely didn't want. But as she slowly began taking steps, crossing the balcony to him, the only thing he could do was open his arms.

The moment she came close, he gathered her to him, needing to hold her. He felt the willpower he had tried to regain slip away. She pressed against him, needing to be held. She wrapped her arms around his neck and they stood that way for a long moment, body to body, soul to soul. Slow warmth spread from her to him and it seemed that her every curve was molded against his firm muscled length.

And then he swooped her up into his arms and with hurried steps carried her back into the bedroom and placed her on the bed. He leaned down and caught her lips in a kiss that was deep, sensual and demanded full surrender. The sounds of pleasure emitting from her made him want her that much more and his stomach clenched with profound need.

He released her to pull the shirt from over her head, and then proceeded to remove his pants. After taking the time to put on protection, he joined her in bed. She whispered his name and the only thing Jared could think about was demonstrating with his body just what she did to him and how much he wanted her.

The knowledge that she wanted him as much as he wanted her sent his desire skyrocketing in all directions. He intended to spend the rest of the night sharing intense passion with the one woman whose name was more than a whisper on his lips. It was a name that was finding a way to his very soul.

Jared's last thought as he captured her mouth with his was that having her seep into his heart was something he could not let happen. No matter what.

Nine

"Thanks for being here, Dana."

Dana gave Jared an assuring smile when he reached out and took her hand in his and tightened his fingers around it as they sat side by side in the hospital's waiting room. His features were solemn and she knew he was worried about the outcome of his mother's surgery. "You don't have to thank me, Jared. I wanted to be here."

She glanced at the clock on the wall. The doctors had indicated it wouldn't be a long procedure and that someone would be out to talk to the family when it was over. Jared's youngest brother, Reggie, had accompanied Mr. Westmoreland downstairs to the coffee shop, and every so often Jared's cell phone would ring when one of his other brothers called for an update on their mother's condition. His aunt and uncle were here and so were several of his cousins and their wives. One thing she had learned about the Westmorelands was that they were a close-knit family who bonded in a crisis. She admired that about them.

Dana glanced up at Jared. "Can I get you anything?"

He gave her a reassuring smile. "No, thanks, I'm fine." He then leaned closer and whispered softly, privately, "What I really want is something I can't have right now, but there's always later."

Dana felt heat flare into her cheeks and hoped no one noticed the blush that came into her features. After returning from Jekyll Island they had begun spending more and more time together. They had dined at his place and gone out to eat a couple of times this week, had taken in several movies and had also joined his cousins last night at Chase's Place to celebrate Thorn's birthday.

And each time they made love it was better than the last. On the nights that he stayed over, she enjoyed waking up in his arms. There were never any regrets, only complete fulfillment. She could not resist Jared any more than she could stop breathing. The intimacy they shared was tangible, special and so profound, that more than once it brought tears to her eyes.

Tonight she was having dinner again at his place and was looking forward to it. She hoped they had reason to celebrate, and remained positive about his mother's condition.

For the next few minutes she tried engaging Jared in small talk since she knew that he, like everyone else, was watching the clock. His father had returned and was now nervously pacing the room.

Everyone looked up when the doctor walked into the

waiting room with an unreadable expression on his face. Mr. Westmoreland, with Jared and Reggie on his heels, quickly walked over to meet the doctor.

"How is she?" James Westmoreland asked in a somewhat shaky voice.

Dr. Miller smiled and he reached out and touched the older man's shoulder. "She's doing fine and test results confirm the lump was nothing but fatty tissue. Sarah is fine and once the anesthesia wears off, she'll be able to leave. Of course I want to see her for a follow-up visit next week."

James sighed deeply and Dana could see relief and happiness in everyone's eyes. "Thanks, Dr. Miller."

"You're welcome." Dr. Miller glanced over at Jared and Reggie. "Which one of you is engaged to be married?"

Jared lifted a brow. "I am. Why?"

The doctor chuckled. "Because that's all your mother talked about from the time they wheeled her into the operating room to right before the anesthetic kicked in. She's really happy about it and is anxious to start planning a wedding. Congratulations." He then turned and walked out of the waiting room.

Jared turned his head and met Dana's gaze. Her fingers tightened on the straps on her purse. It was an unconscious gesture that only he noticed. She had agreed to play out this charade for an additional two weeks, but he understood how everything was placing a toll on her. It was placing a hell of a toll on him as well.

He studied her face, knowing that even after their "engagement" ended, memories would remain that wouldn't leave him alone, that were bound to creep into his thoughts at any place and at any time.

He sighed deeply as he crossed the room to where Dana was standing, needing the contact, the closeness. "Mom's fine," he said.

Her smile was soft. "I heard and I'm glad," she said so quietly that he barely heard her.

Elated with the news that his mother was okay, and because he was dying to taste Dana's lips, Jared bent his head and brushed his lips across hers.

"If you two keep this up, your Mom's prediction is bound to be true," James said, grinning, coming to stand beside his oldest son.

Another deep sigh escaped Jared's lips. He had an idea but knew he was expected to ask, so he did. "And what prediction is that?"

Mr. Westmoreland looked at Dana then back at his son and chuckled. "That there will be another Westmoreland wedding before the end of summer."

Dana had fallen in love with Jared's home the first time she had walked through the double doors a week ago. The two-story structure, located in one of North Atlanta's most exclusive and affluent communities, was huge and spacious.

When Jared had given her a tour she'd seen that each and every room was breathtaking and expensively decorated, and that included the state-of-the-art theater room she had heard so much about, and a beautifully designed swimming pool. He had five bedrooms, six bathrooms, a huge country kitchen, a living room and dining room as well as a breakfast room, a library and game room. He even had a four-car garage and she had been surprised to discover that he owned a motorcycle.

He had explained that because of Thorn, all the male Westmorelands owned a Thorn-Byrd, the brand of bikes that his cousin built.

The house, Dana thought, was very much like the man who owned it, fascinating, interesting and compelling. With all the vaulted ceilings, rich thick carpeting, costly paintings that lined the walls and the expensive antique furnishings, it signified wealth but wasn't overdone. There was nothing ostentatious about the house or the man. It was obvious that Jared liked nice things, but she definitely wouldn't consider his likes eccentric or outlandish.

"Make yourself comfortable," Jared said as he glanced over at her. It was early evening. They had spent the majority of the day at his parents' home after his mother had gotten released from the hospital. He had made all the necessary calls to his brothers, assuring them that things were fine and their mother was okay.

"Do you need my help?" Dana asked as she sat at the breakfast bar and watched how efficiently he moved around in the kitchen.

"No. We're having something light and simple."

Dana chuckled. "Umm, let me guess, hot dogs and lemonade?"

Jared smiled. "No, it's something a lot more filling than that. In fact it's one of the few Westmoreland family secret recipes that Chase will share—a chicken-and-rice casserole. I prepared it this morning before leaving for the hospital, so all I have to do is warm it up. I'm also making a salad to go along with it and thought a glass of wine would be nice, as well."

She watched as he pulled a casserole dish from the refrigerator and proceeded to place it in the microwave. He then pulled out all the items he needed for the salad.

"And you're sure there's nothing I can do to help?" The last time she had shared a dinner with him here, he'd had everything catered.

He glanced up at her and smiled. "I'm positive. You've done enough already. I meant what I said about me appreciating you taking off work to be at the hospital today. It meant a lot to me and I know it meant a lot to my family, especially Mom. I'm so thankful that the test results were good. In a way I had prepared myself for the worse."

Dana heard the catch in his voice and immediately got out of her seat and came around to stand in front of him. She reached out and placed a hand on his arm. "But like you said, Jared, the results were good and that's what's important. She's okay."

Jared nodded and thought that Dana's touch felt hot on his arm. A seductive silence hung over the room as he held her gaze. Desire swirled around in his belly and he hung tenuously on to his control. He wanted her. Always wanted her. Constantly wanted her. And was always amazed at the depth of that wanting.

He recalled vividly and in living color every aspect of making love to her last night. They had returned to her place from the movies, and as soon as the door closed shut behind them, desire, the likes of which he'd never encountered before, had taken hold of him, racked his mind, rammed through his body. He had hauled her to him, picked her up into his arms and had taken her into the bedroom where he had stripped her of her clothes, and then quickly removed his own, barely taking time to protect them both before covering her body with his and making love to her.

The same way he wanted to make love to her now.

He made a move to reach out for her the exact moment the alarm on the microwave sounded. Inhaling deeply, a faint smile formed on his lips. "I guess it's time to eat."

She smiled in return. "Yes, I guess it is."

"Will you go swimming with me?" Jared asked later when they had finished dinner, cleared the table and loaded the dishes in the dishwasher. The last time she'd been over, the lining of the pool was being redone.

She slanted him a teasing grin. "What makes you think I can swim?"

He regarded her with an interest that had her toes curling and the most intimate part of her aching. "I just figured you could, and if you can't then I'll teach you."

Her eyes squinted with amusement. "You're an expert swimmer?"

"I don't do so bad."

Dana thought that if he could swim with the same degree of expertise that he made love then he was definitely an ace. "I can swim," she said, deciding to come clean. "My parents made sure I knew how before my fourth birthday. Living on the East Coast and so close to the ocean meant that I had to learn."

She tipped her head back and looked at him. "But there is one slight problem."

"What?"

"I didn't bring a bathing suit."

"That's no problem. I'm sure there's an extra one around here that should fit you."

He watched her face and saw the exact moment her eyes darkened with disappointment. "Don't bother."

He quickly realized what had bothered her. Reaching out he gently squeezed her shoulders and said, "It's a bathing suit that Delaney left behind, Dana. She used to keep several of them here in case she ever wanted to visit and go swimming." He pulled her to him, needing to hold her. "I've never gone swimming with a woman in this house before," he whispered. He never felt the need to explain his personal life to any woman, but for some reason he wanted to explain things to her.

Dana pulled back, ticked at herself for caring. Besides, he didn't owe her an explanation about anything. It wasn't as if they were really engaged. "Sorry, I don't have a right to come across like that, Jared. What you do is none of my business."

He studied her face for a long time then said, "There's no need to apologize." His breath was warm against her face when he leaned toward her and placed a gentle kiss on her lips. He deepened it then pulled back slowly, not ready to languish her lips yet as he placed tiny kisses around it. "I can say the hell with a bathing suit and let's go skinny-dipping."

Breathless, she smiled against his lips. "Yes, you can say that but then that poses another problem."

He watched as she moistened her lips with a stroke of her tongue, and was tempted to lean down and take that tongue into his mouth and feast on it some more. "What other problem?" he asked, barely able to get the words out.

"I've never swum in the nude."

The thought of her swimming naked ran fluidly through his mind, forming images that made him want to strip her bare, then and there. "You know what they say, Miss Rollins. There's a first time for everything." He leaned down and whispered in her ear, "Come on, let's go for a swim."

When they began walking, Jared slung an arm around her shoulders as he led her to the area where the pool was located. Dana tried not to let the seductive sensations that Jared generated within her, take possession of her mind.

The potent smell of chlorine teased Dana's nostrils as they entered a passageway. He reached out and flipped a switch, bringing light into a huge area filled with lush greenery. To say the pool was impressive would be an understatement. Secured in the privacy of brick walls and a vaulted ceiling made of solid glass, this private place was definitely a swimmer's haven. Dana smiled when they stopped walking and she looked up and saw how the moonlight and the stars reflected through, slanting light against the pool's blue-tinted waters.

"So, do you want a bathing suit or do you prefer going without?" Jared asked as he placed his hands on her hips.

She grinned. "I think I'd feel more comfortable with a bathing suit."

He watched her thoughtfully, wondering if this was the same woman who had played a very enticing game of hide-and-seek with him that weekend. It had been one passionate pursuit and now it seemed that she was trying to go all shy on him. However he was sure a few sizzling kisses would rid her of any degree of bashfulness.

"I may as well warn you that I plan to take the suit off of you the first chance I get," he whispered, leaning down and capturing her earlobe in his mouth and sucking gently.

A breathless sigh escaped Dana's lips and she closed her eyes. It was a good thing he was still holding her by the waist or she would have melted and slid right into the pool. "I kind of figured you'd be trying something like that."

He took her hand in his and drew her away from the pool to an area surrounded by a bevy of palm trees. "At least I gave you fair warning."

He led her to a room off from the pool area that appeared to be a large dressing room. "You can change in here," Jared said, giving her an easy smile. "Towels are in that closet and there's a bathing suit that should fit you in that drawer over there."

She looked up at him. "What about you?"

He gave her that same grin that had endeared him to her the first time she'd seen it. "I don't have a problem swimming in the nude, Dana."

And with that he turned and left her alone in the room.

Dana nervously fumbled with the buttons on her blouse as she removed it while glancing around the huge room. She saw that all the walls and the ceiling were mirrored and she felt slightly funny as she watched herself undress. She studied the daybed that sat on one side of the room and didn't want to imagine Jared and some woman in it as they watched themselves make love. He had said no woman had ever gone swimming with him in this house but who was to say that no woman had ever made out with him in this room?

Letting out a long breath, she tugged her skirt down over her hips, not wanting the picture of Jared and any other woman to form in her mind. As she'd told him, what he did was his business. But still, the part of her that loved him so much that it hurt, felt pain at the thought of him with someone else.

She tried turning her thoughts and attention elsewhere. Dinner had been delicious and the wine he'd selected had been perfect.

She could tell a huge load had been lifted off his shoulders now that he knew his mother was okay. He seemed more relaxed. Being around him made her feel things, want things and each and every time he had smiled at her, touched her—innocently or otherwise—she found herself hard pressed to keep her emotions under control.

Whenever she looked into his eyes his keen sense of intelligence startled her. He was his parents' firstborn, but had not been the heir apparent. Anything and everything Jared possessed was the result of hard work. He deserved all he had achieved and was a man like no other she'd ever known. There was a fierceness about him, yet at the same time an innate gentleness that she found sweet and endearing.

Jared Westmoreland was the man she would love until the day she died.

Dana sighed, as she tied her hair back, trying to remain clearheaded. She couldn't and wouldn't have regrets, no matter what. And she wouldn't dwell on the impossibilities of a future with Jared.

Moments later she glanced at herself in the mirror. Jared had said nothing about the bathing suit being a bikini. It appeared to be brand-new and was a perfect fit, although it showed more skin than she was used to exposing. Jared had seen her naked several times since their weekend together, but for some reason she felt shy around him tonight.

Maybe it was because every time she held his gaze for any period of time she saw desire in his eyes that was so thick it could be cut with a knife. And what he'd said earlier about her not keeping the bathing suit on for long sent passionate chills down her body. He'd said it and she had no reason to doubt it. Grabbing a towel she wrapped it securely around her waist and took a deep breath before walking out of the room.

The first thing she noticed was that Jared had dimmed the lights. The second thing was that he was already in the water, standing in the shallow end, leaning back against the pool's wall. All the way across the room she could feel the strength of him. Knowing he was completely naked only filled her with heated passion and desire. He was built and had the kind of muscles women drooled about. Each and every time she came into contact with his body, she burned.

"Get rid of the towel, Dana."

His words as well as the look in his eyes pulled her to him. She slowly walked to the edge of the pool and met his heated gaze. "And if I don't?"

A smile touched the corners of his lips. "Then I'll be

tempted to get out of the pool and remove it for you, and while I'm removing the towel I'll also remove everything else."

Dana tilted her head, picturing both things in her mind. "Mmm, that sounds like quite a seductive threat, Counselor."

She watched as he moved swiftly and agilely through the water and ended up at the side of the pool, within less than a few feet from where she stood. "No threat, Dana. It's a promise."

She took a step back when he eased his naked body out of the pool. She noticed he had on a condom, making it blatantly clear what he had in mind. Dripping wet he stood in front of her. He leaned over and kissed her tenderly while at the same time used his fingertip to loosen the knot of the towel. She felt it fall to the floor, but his mouth kept her too occupied to care. At the moment she was content to let him carry out any threats he'd made.

"You look nice," he said huskily, releasing her lips and letting his gaze roam over her body. "You're definitely wearing this bathing suit—but not for long."

With a flick of his wrist he released her top and then bending, he caressed her bare shoulders with the tip of his tongue. That was followed by slow nibbling kisses that he placed on her neck before moving to her breasts, taking the hard tips of her nipples into his mouth one at a time.

When she began to shudder he slowly lowered himself down in front of her and began easing the bikini bottom down her legs.

"Your body leaves me breathless, Dana," he whispered as his lips trailed kisses all over her stomach. "And your scent drives me crazy."

His mouth moved downward and he reached out and gently grabbed hold of her hips. Glancing up at her and seeing how she watched everything he was doing while taking measured breaths and gripping his shoulders for balance, he said, "I love kissing you all over."

He felt a shiver flow through her body and whispered huskily, "But I especially love kissing you here."

He heard her moan when his mouth closed over her most intimate part, finding her hot and wet. His tongue flicked out and began stroking her slowly and tasting her completely. When she arched against his mouth, he became greedy, insistent and possessive.

"Jared!"

She screamed his name. He felt her buckle against his mouth as every sensitive nerve in her body exploded. He wanted it all and he didn't let up until her last shudder ended and she became soft and limp. Standing, he swept her into his arms and carried her over to a huge padded bench and held her. Placing her in his lap he tightened his hold on her and drew her closer, needing the contact and not wanting to question the why of it.

"You're too much, Jared," Dana whispered on a half sigh, barely opening her eyes.

His smile was intriguing. "Is that a bad thing or a good thing?"

"Umm, I imagine it's a good thing," she said softly.

His chuckle was soft and the sound of it sent more sensual chills up Dana's body. "You imagine? You're not certain?"

She hooked her arms around his neck. "Give me a few moments to recoup and I'll let you know for sure."

"You don't have a few moments to spare, sweetheart. I want you too much," he said throatily. And then he was kissing her again, his lips hungry, his tongue hot, intense. Her body immediately responded and began to heat up all over again.

He slowly pulled back. "Come on, let's swim for a while."

He stood with her in his arms and walked over to the pool. "The water is temperature controlled, so it's warm."

They eased their bodies into the pool. After treading water for a few moments, they swam to the other side of the pool then back again. Going to the edge of the pool he gathered her close. Before she could gasp her next breath, he kissed her, touched her all over and completely shattered her sanity.

Mindlessly, she moaned his name when his finger slipped inside of her, stroking her to heated bliss. "Wrap your legs around my waist."

Meeting his gaze she placed her arms around his neck, and when he positioned her body just where he wanted it he slowly eased inside of her, finding she was still moist and hot.

And when he had gone as deep as he could go, Jared's head came down and moments before he covered her lips he whispered the words, "This is as perfect as anything can possibly get."

And then he began moving inside of her, making love to her, taking, giving and sharing. Water lapped against their skin, absorbing the heat of their naked flesh, stroking their passion to a fevered pitch.

It seemed as if it had been months, years since they had shared passion this way and all the longings Dana could possibly endure broke through, encasing her in a storm of emotions and pleasures that ripped through to her very soul. And when he increased the rhythm, she pressed closer to him, urged him to take more as passion swirled around her, driving her through turbulence that could only have one end. Each stroke he made pushed her closer and closer to release. She dug her fingers into his shoulders as liquid warmth gathered, anticipation hovered and pleasure crested.

Jared let out a deep guttural groan when he felt a shudder race through Dana's body and she ground her hips against him, pushing him deeper inside of her, to the hilt. And then he lost it, that final, fragile hold on his sanity. His next powerful thrust connected them in a way that made sensations shoot through both of them simultaneously. Blood pounded in his ears and her name trembled from his lips at the same time that his body shook in a release so strong that he was whirled into a massive impact that stole his next breath.

He felt Dana tremble in his arms, her response shameless, total and complete. The effects tore through him, ripped him in two and demanded that he give up everything, all that he had, whatever he possessed, to the fury of passion that consumed them both.

And as he crushed her to him, he surrendered to the multitude of feelings that drew them together. *She was his.*

Ten

"**I** want my wife back, Jared. She refuses to see me or talk to me so what do you suggest that I do?"

Jared sighed deeply wondering how Sylvester expected him to answer a question like that when he had his own personal issues to deal with. It had been almost two weeks since his mother's surgery and tonight was the night of Thorn and Tara's anniversary party—and the final act of the play in which he and Dana had been participants. They were supposed to officially end things tonight by breaking their engagement.

"Jared? Are you listening to me?"

Jared turned his attention back to his client who'd been pacing his office for the past half hour. Evidently, Sylvester thought that as his attorney Jared had all the answers, which was a completely false assumption. He was in the business of ending marriages and not trying to find ways to save them.

"Have you tried begging?" Jared decided to ask. The last time he had spoken with Jackie Brewster's attorney, he'd been informed that she was adamant about giving her husband the divorce he'd asked for. She refused to remain married to a man who had wrongly accused her of being unfaithful.

Sylvester frowned. "I'm serious, Jared."

"So am I. According to your wife's attorney, she wants us to proceed. She says there's no chance of reconciliation."

Sylvester, with a defeated expression on his face, dropped down in a nearby chair. "I can't lose her. I love her, Jared, and I will do whatever I have to do to save my marriage. I was wrong. I knew what a good woman she was, yet I was quick to think the worst. It was so hard to accept that someone could actually love me and give me their complete devotion."

Behind his desk, Jared leaned back in his chair. It was odd to watch Sylvester this torn up over a woman. In the past, he'd been quick to end things and move on, usually because he had some other woman waiting in the wings. But that wasn't the case this time. It was obvious Sylvester was in love with his wife.

Love.

With that one word, Dana quickly came into his thoughts. He blinked, refusing to go there. What he felt for her was desire, gut-wrenching desire, lust of the strongest kind. He'd been in relationships before and was an ace at getting out of them whenever things got sticky. And he would be the first to admit that things between him and Dana were definitely getting sticky. It was time to split—with no regrets.

"Isn't there something you can do, Jared? I'm desperate."

Sylvester's words recaptured his attention. He stared up at the ceiling in deep thought for a moment. "Maybe there is," he said, making a quick decision. "I'll do my best to arrange for you and Jackie to have a private meeting, without me or her attorney present. I can't make any promises, but I'll try. Once the two of you are alone, it's going to be up to you to convince her that you're worthy of forgiveness."

He saw the hopeful gleam that appeared in Sylvester's eyes and the optimism that lined the man's features. It was evident he was struggling to hold on to his composure. If there had been any doubt in Jared's mind of just how deeply Sylvester felt about his wife, it vanished at that very moment.

"Are you okay, Dana?" Cybil asked, studying her best friend's face.

Dana looked up from the papers on her desk and forced a smile. "Yes, I'm fine." She quickly glanced away, knowing she couldn't hide her emotions from Cybil.

"If you're fine then why have you been crying?"

Dana began studying the papers on her desk again. "Who says I've been crying?"

"I do," Cybil said quietly, crossing the room to stand in front of Dana's desk. When seconds ticked by and Dana didn't say anything, Cybil spoke again, her voice low and imploring. "I didn't want you to get hurt."

Dana slowly stood from her desk and walked over to the window. She stared out until she was certain that her voice wouldn't tremble with each word she was about to say. "I didn't get hurt. I enjoyed each and every moment I spent with Jared."

"And you fell head over heels in love with him," Cybil said, stating the obvious.

Dana met Cybil's concerned gaze. "Yes, I fell in love with him. I didn't mean for it to happen, but it did. I love Jared with all my heart and I don't have any regrets about it."

Cybil crossed the room to stand in front of Dana. "All right. Now what?"

Dana looked away, to glance back out the window. "Now we've come to the end of our road. Tonight we end things and tomorrow I go back to being an unengaged woman."

Pain settled deep in Dana's heart. How could she go back to the solitary life she'd known after being with Jared for the past six weeks? Not only with Jared, but with all the Westmorelands. For a little while, they had filled a need in her she hadn't realized existed—a need to belong to a family. It was going to be hard going back to being alone again.

"Ben and I are going to the Amelia Islands in the morning to attend the tennis tournament. Come with us."

Dana gave Cybil a reassuring smile. "I'll be fine. I will survive." She chuckled. "It won't be my first broken engagement," she said teasingly.

"But it will be the one that really mattered—pretense or not."

Dana nodded. "Yes, it will be the one that mattered."

"And will you be ready for the questions on Monday? The speculations? The gossip?"

On a long sigh Dana ran her hand through her hair. No, she wouldn't be ready for any of that but she would deal with it. She gave a wry smile. "I'm ready for whatever comes my way, Cybil."

But she knew the moment she'd said the words that they were a lie.

"Why do I get the feeling that you're not in a good mood tonight?"

Jared gave his cousin Storm a crooked smile and lifted the glass of punch to his lips, took a sip and then asked. "I don't know. Why do you?"

A chuckle escaped Storm's lips. "I've often heard if you want a straight answer, then don't ask an attorney a question."

"Yes, I've heard that one, too," Jared said, giving his cousin a wink and taking another sip of his punch. He glanced around, seeing all the people who had shown up to celebrate Thorn and Tara's first wedding anniversary. Even after a year, the thought of Thorn being married was still hard to get used to. Jared never thought there was a woman alive who was brave enough to put up with the surly Thorn Westmoreland. Evidently he'd been wrong. Tara seemed to be handling his prickly cousin very well and it didn't take much to see how in love they were.

Storm's marriage six months ago had been another surprise, and Jared couldn't help but dwell on all the changes that had taken place in Storm's life since then. The man who had once been Atlanta's most sought-after bachelor, who had been known as *The Perfect Storm* to multitudes of women, the man who swore he would never, ever marry was now a happily married man with a wife and twins on the way.

"What happened?" Jared asked. He suddenly needed answers and he'd force them out of Storm if necessary.

Storm raised a dark brow. "What do you mean what happened?"

"With you and this marriage thing. You swore you would never fall in love but you did and I want to know what happened."

A huge smile stretched Storm's lips. "Since you're engaged to be married yourself, I don't understand the need for this cross-examination. But just in case for some reason the verdict's still out, or you're attempting to find logic in all of this, the answer is simple. Love happened. I met a woman who I couldn't live without. At first I thought it was strictly physical since there was such a strong attraction between us, but then I discovered there was more to it than just being intimate. I enjoyed being with her, going places with her, seeing her smile and sharing my thoughts with her. And she was different from any woman I'd ever known."

Storm chuckled before continuing. "It took me a while to rationalize the depth of my feelings but when I did, I knew just what I wanted and who I wanted. And I also knew what I could lose if I didn't accept the truth and act on those feelings. I needed Jayla in my life, as part of my life, just as much as I needed to breathe."

Jared's troubled gaze met Storm's. "You were vulnerable."

Storm shook his head. "That's a subjective viewpoint, Jared, but also a wrong one. I was in love. I was so deeply entrenched in the throes of it that there was no way I could walk away. Jayla has added meaning to my life in ways I didn't think possible. But then from what I can tell, Dana has done the same for you. It shows every time the two of you are together. I've never seen you this attentive to any woman. For the past ten minutes you've been standing here getting agitated as you wait for her to return from touring the house with Tara. You love her, man. I thought I had it bad, but you have it worse. Hell, you're in worse shape than Thorn was and he hadn't known he was in love with Tara until it was almost too late."

Jared took another sip of his drink. He wondered what his cousin would say if he were to tell him he was wrong, that he wasn't in love with Dana, and that the entire engagement had been nothing but a sham.

Whatever he was about to say died on his lips the moment Dana walked through the patio doors with Tara. Tara and Thorn had had the house built and had moved into it a few months ago. It was a beautiful structure located in the outskirts of town on land that had been in the Westmoreland family for generations.

"Well, there's your lady, Jared. And if you're as smart as I know you are, whatever doubt that's beginning to form in your mind will soon vanish. Dana is a treasure worth having and if I were you I'd go a step further than just putting a ring on her finger. I'd make her officially mine as soon as I could."

"And what about the risk?"

Storm's eyes came swiftly to his. "What risk?"

"Divorce."

Storm shook his head. "You've been handling way too many divorce cases, Jared. When you're in love, you don't think of failure, you only think of success and prosperity. Life is full of risks. Each time I leave the station and head out to fight a fire there's a risk. You don't dwell on the what-ifs, and you have to believe that some risks are definitely worth taking. You have to believe in forever. And with that," Storm said, setting down his glass on the table beside him, "I think I'll go find my wife and give her a huge kiss."

Jared lifted his forehead. "Why?

Storm gave him a smart-ass grin. "No particular reason. Just because."

Jared watched as Storm walked away before switching his attention back to Dana. She met his gaze and smiled. He smiled back then sighed deeply as he thought of how right things seemed at that moment. From the first, Dana had blended well with his family. And when she stood in a group with his female cousins, as she was doing now, she seemed so much a part of the Westmorelands. It seemed perfectly right for her to be here with them and with him.

As he continued to hold her gaze he suddenly knew that everything Storm had said was true. As much as he wanted to deny it and *had* denied it, the truth was now crystal clear. He *was* in love. He wanted and needed Dana in his life.

He wanted forever.

How many times in the last six weeks had he reminded himself that their engagement was nothing but pretense? That no matter how much he enjoyed being with her, the time would come for it to end, and for him to go back to playing the field with flashy women who weren't looking for commitment? All the while knowing that his life would become empty without Dana in it.

How many times had he longed to keep things the way they were, but convinced himself that he didn't want or need a woman in his life? That he had seen the ugly side of marriage too much to take the risks for himself? But Storm was right. Some risks were worth taking.

The thought of Dana with someone else, sharing what they had shared was unacceptable. When they had entered into this pretense, he'd had no intention of letting his guard down around her. But he had. And she had eased her way into his heart as easily as anything he'd ever seen. He'd tried to put up resistance, had told himself countless times what he'd felt for her was nothing but lust. However, he knew just as sure as he was standing here that what he felt for her was love of the richest kind and if he was completely honest, he could even admit he had probably fallen in love with her the moment she'd stormed into his office. From that day on, he had wanted her with a passion unlike anything he'd ever felt before.

He wondered what Dana wanted. Was there a chance that she had feelings for him? Could she love him? There was only one way to find out. If she loved him, too, it would definitely make things a lot easier, and if she didn't, then he would just have to take the same advice he'd given Sylvester earlier that day. He would beg if he had to, because he had no intention of letting

Dana go. Whether it was using reason or resorting to seduction, he would do what he had to do to win Dana's heart forever.

Dana didn't have to ask Jared if he wanted to come in when he took her home that night. She wanted him to and hoped that he would. Tonight was their last night together and she wanted one more lasting memory. Besides, she needed to give him back his ring.

When she had returned from touring Tara and Thorn's house she had noticed something different about Jared. It wasn't anything that she could put her finger on, but she sensed something was up. He'd always been attentive when they were together, but tonight it seemed that he was doubly so. And for someone who was supposed to announce to his family that they had broken their engagement tomorrow, he seemed too much the adoring, doting fiancé tonight for such a thing to be believable. There had been the hand holding and the loving kisses that all painted a picture of a couple who were very much in love.

And then there were the times she had caught him looking at her, sometimes in the oddest way. Once, when their gazes had locked, without warning and right in the middle of Dare's conversation, Jared had cupped her face in his hand and kissed her in front of his family, slowly and firmly, before whispering the words, "Let's leave," seductively in her ear.

So here they were, back at her place and as he closed the door behind them she wondered what he had in mind. But whatever it was, she was determined not to lose her composure. She would get through this night as they said their goodbyes.

"It was a nice party, wasn't it?" she asked, trying to generate conversation.

Jared leaned against the door, saying nothing as he watched her with intense dark eyes. "Yes, it was nice."

"And that motorcycle that Thorn presented to Tara was beautiful, simply awesome. To think he made it with his own hands. I can't imagine all the hours it took for him to do it. That was such a special gift to her."

"Yes, it was."

"It's obvious they are so happy together," she added, knowing she had started to ramble. "It's plain to see how much in love they are."

Jared smiled. "Yes, it is. In fact all my cousins who've gotten married appear to be happily in love."

She met his gaze. "What about Chase? Do you think he'll follow his brothers into matrimony eventually?"

Jared eased away from the door to stand in front of her. "Yes, I think he will, once he finds the right woman."

Dana nodded. She wondered if Jared would ever change his mind about love and marriage or if he would always let what he saw in his profession dictate how his future would be.

Knowing there was something she couldn't put off doing any longer, she let out a long, shaky breath as she lifted her hand and eased the engagement ring from her finger. She handed it to him. "It's time to give this back."

He shook his head as his gaze continued to hold hers. He took the ring from her and placed it back on her finger. "No, I want you to keep it."

She blinked. "I can't do that," she said incredulously, shocked he would suggest such a thing.

"Why not? You wanted to keep Cord's ring."

"But only because I was stuck with all those wedding expenses. Pretending to be engaged to you hasn't cost me anything," she said softly, not wanting to admit that it *had* cost her something. Her heart.

He didn't say anything for a few moments and then he gently took her into his arms and gathered her close. He pulled back briefly, met her gaze and in Dana's mind he was looking at her the same way he had done earlier that night.

She held his gaze and every emotion Dana could think of took hold of her. Every time she thought about the fact that this would be the last time they shared together, that chances were when he walked out the door he wouldn't be coming back, despair took hold of her. But she refused to let their last night together end in gloom and doom. It hadn't started out that way and she wouldn't let it end that way.

Jared leaned down and their mouths joined. Immediately, Dana could tell there was something different about this kiss. It still packed a lot of passion that sent toe-curling sensations through her, but there was a degree of tenderness that touched her deeply, almost brought tears to her eyes. It was as if he was methodically placing his stamp on her.

Moments later when he drew away, she had to hold on to his hand to keep her balance. She could actually hear her heart pounding.

"Let's play one final game," Jared whispered softly.

"A final game?" she asked, thinking of the two others they had played together. Her heart began pounding even harder just thinking about them. And the purely seductive male look in his eyes wasn't helping matters.

He looked at her for several long, quiet moments, then said, "Yes. Let's play Truth or Dare?"

With a sigh, Dana looked down at her hands, her gaze focused on the ring he had placed back there. She looked up at him. "I haven't played that in years, since high school at a sleepover."

"Then you know how it's played?"

"Yes." But something told her that Jared would have his own version of the game. What would his dare be like? And did she really want to bare her heart and soul by telling him the truth about anything he asked?

Jared kept his gaze leveled on her. "Okay then let's get started. You go first," he murmured softly.

Dana heaved a deep breath. "Truth or dare?" she challenged.

A smile spread from Jared's lips to his entire face. "Truth."

"Okay." She paused for a moment, wondering what she could ask him and decided to go easy. "What did you enjoy the most about Thorn and Tara's party tonight?"

"Being there with you."

Dana's breath caught and goose bumps formed on her arms with his response. She hadn't expected him to say that. Before she could recover he said, "Truth or dare?"

She decided she would stick with the truth. "Truth."

"What did *you* enjoy the most about the party tonight?" he asked.

Dana sighed. She had hoped he wouldn't ask her that. She had enjoyed a lot about the party tonight, but she knew what she'd enjoyed the most. She met his gaze and told him the truth. "The moment you kissed me in front of everyone."

She saw the darkening of Jared's eyes. She heard the deepening of his breathing. Both sparked desires within her. He reached out and touched her chin, and then his finger moved slowly down the center of her neck to where her pulse was pounding. "Truth or dare," she challenged again, barely able to get the words out.

Although it was impossible, it seemed his eyes darkened more. "Dare," he said huskily.

Dana swallowed past the lump, especially with Jared's hand still there on her neck, drawing lazy circles with his fingers, stimulating both her mind and her body. She could only think of one dare at the moment. "I dare you to kiss me like I'm the only woman you could ever want." A part of Dana knew how badly that must have sounded, but it was her dare and she wondered what he would do about it.

Jared felt his groin tighten in response to Dana's dare. He doubted that she knew how beautiful and sexy she looked, waiting to see what he would do. Fulfilling her dare wasn't a problem since in his mind she was the only woman he could ever want anyway. But she didn't know it and maybe it was about time she did.

He reached out and gently pulled her to him. There was no waiting, and his mouth took hers with all the urgency and need that he felt. He heard her whimper the moment his tongue entered her mouth, and as he began mating his mouth with hers, he felt the shiver that ran down her body. He had kissed her a number of times, but now he was kissing her as the woman he had singled out to spend the rest of his life with, and he was determined to let it show in his kiss. All evening he had longed to kiss her this way. That kiss in front of his family was merely meant to tide him over until now. Until this. His heart was filled with love and his body was wired with sensuous need. Together, both were causing him to overload.

When she grabbed the back of his head, locking their mouths, his hand eased under her blouse, unhooked the front catch to her bra to touch her breasts. Her felt the tips hardened beneath his fingers, felt her body's response to it in her kiss. She moaned in his mouth and the sound sent fire through every nerve in his body. Then when breathing became a necessity, he slowly pulled back, reluctantly breaking off the kiss.

Dana swallowed a frustrated groan. She hadn't wanted him to stop kissing her. Thanks to him she knew how it felt to come apart in a man's arms. She'd discovered all the pleasure a person could experience in making love.

"Truth or dare?"

A heated flutter floated around in her chest, a tingling sensation took root in her stomach. She nervously bit her bottom lip, looked up at him and met his gaze and said, "Dare."

He smiled, seemingly pleased. Then said, "Give me your underwear."

Dana blinked, wondered if she'd heard him right, although she knew that she had. The room felt charged when she lifted her skirt. The heat in his gaze intensified and her breathing pattern became irregular.

Holding his gaze, she slowly eased her bikini panties down her legs. When they were completely off, she balled them up in her hand and handed them to him.

He took them. "Thanks."

Now it was her turn. "Truth or Dare?"

His deep penetrating gaze met hers. "Dare."

A wicked gleam appeared in her eyes when she said, "Give me yours."

Jared chuckled quietly as his hands went to his belt and he pulled it out of the loop. Next he eased down his zipper. Dana watched as he removed his jeans, then the pair of black briefs he was wearing. She inhaled deeply when he stood before her naked from the waist down. Completely naked and totally aroused.

He held her gaze. "Truth or Dare."

She gave him an intimate smile. "Dare."

"I dare you to take off the rest of your clothes."

Dana's heart began beating faster as she began unbuttoning her blouse to take if off. She then removed her bra that was half off anyway. Next was the skirt that she eased down her legs along with her half slip. Her body shivered at the intense desire she saw in Jared's gaze as he looked at her. His eyes seemed fixated with the area below her navel.

"Truth or Dare?" she asked softly, feeling totally exposed, yet at the same time, utterly sexy while standing nude before him.

"Dare," he said throatily, as if that one word had been torn from deep inside his throat.

She nodded, wondering if they would ever get back to truths when it was much more fun being daring. Just looking at him standing in her living room more naked than dressed, made her feel warm, wet and wanton. "Take off the rest of yours, as well."

All he had to do was pull his shirt over his head and

he was done. "Truth or Dare?" he challenged in a husky voice as his gaze moved down the length of her. She felt her body burn everywhere his eyes touched. She also felt her blood simmer slowly through each of her veins.

"Truth," she responded, letting out a slow breath.

"Now that we're naked, what do you want us to do?" he asked. The magnitude of desire in his eyes had her body burning.

She held his gaze. They were back to the truth again. Everything feminine within her yearned for him, actually ached. The area between her legs was throbbing unmercifully. And she could think of only one way to end the torment. "I want you to make love to me. Here. Now. And don't hold back on anything."

Her words were both a truth and a dare, Jared thought, as he filled with need and desire, and an overpowering love slammed into him. Something within him snapped and he wanted to give her exactly what she'd asked for.

He reached out, pulled her to him and kissed her, drowning in the sweet moistness of her mouth. He wanted to touch her, taste her, mark her as his. And although he knew such a thing wasn't possible, he wanted to seduce her into loving him as much as he loved her.

He tugged her down on the carpeted floor and let out a low growl of need when he left her mouth to devour the rest of her. His tongue was hot and the skin it tasted increased the fever and the hunger inside him. And Dana wasn't helping matters. Her hands were touching him everywhere, letting him know that she was driven by the same fierce urgency. When she took him into her hand, running her fingers down his hot, slick shaft, he sucked in his breath. She was burning for him the same way he was on fire for her and he knew of only one way to put out the flames.

"No more," he said, pushing aside her hands, his arousal beyond the point of control. He quickly covered her body and entered her, sheathing himself deep. Breathing raggedly, he began thrusting inside of her, holding her gaze as he moved in and out, mating with her like a man who was about to take his last breath and this was the only thing that could sustain him.

Dana followed Jared's frantic rhythm, kept up with his nonstop pace and sucked in a breath at the impact of each and every thrust. Pleasure tore through her relentlessly, urged her to wrap her legs around his hips and pull him deeper inside of her. She wanted this, had asked for it. And he was giving it to her.

"Jared!"

She gave herself to him in torrid abandonment. Shudders, unyielding and unrelenting, rammed through every part of her body, from the top of her head to the tip of her toes. A mass of sensations bombarded the area between her legs where their bodies were joined. And when he picked up the pace, increased the already frantic rhythm, and deepened his steady thrusts, she lifted her body off the floor, needing and wanting everything he had to give.

"Dana!"

Jared's body shook with the force of an orgasm that shot him into ecstasy, filled him with wondrous sensations. A deep guttural growl of satisfaction ripped from deep within his throat and he felt his body explode inside of her. He never knew, never even thought that making love to a woman could be so climactic and earth-shattering, until he'd made love with her. He had never before mated this wildly with a woman, never before wished the rapture would never end.

A short while later, he collapsed on the floor beside her and pulled her into his arms. He wrapped his arms around her as she lay sprawled lifelessly across his chest, the hunger they had for each other satisfied.

"Truth or dare?" she whispered, pressing her lips against the hollow of his throat and gently sucking there.

His breath caught and he felt himself getting hard all over again. "Truth," he said when he was able to breathe normally again.

"What are you thinking?" she asked, somehow finding strength to lean up and stare down at him.

His heart reacted immediately to her question. "I'm thinking that what we just shared is amazing, and that every time we've made love was incredible. I also think that you're beautiful, sexy and a woman any man would want to claim as his. And that I want you in all the ways a man could possibly want a woman. In bed and out of bed. I'm also thinking about the fact that we didn't use protection, but I'm not bothered by it because I don't want things to end between us tonight."

Dana lightly traced her fingers through the hair on his chest. Was he trying to say he wanted her as a lover? That things didn't have to be over after tonight? But how would he explain to his family as to why she had gone from being his fiancée to nothing more than his lover. But then another part of her knew she wanted more from Jared, a lot more than he was willing to give. She refused to sell herself short and it was best to walk away now to save herself heartbreak later.

"Truth or dare, Dana?"

His challenge interrupted her thoughts. She looked at him. "Truth."

He reached out and captured her hand. "What are you thinking?"

She inhaled deeply, then released a slow, shaky breath. "I'm thinking that I can't settle for an affair with you, Jared."

"That's good because I don't want an affair."

At the confused look that appeared on her face, he sat up and pulled her to him and placed a slow, lingering kiss on her lips. When he released her he said, "I want something more than an affair, Dana. I want you to be the woman I come home to every night."

She frowned, not sure she understood what he was saying. "I don't understand."

With a shuddering sigh he said, "Then maybe it's time to put all game playing aside and speak only the truth."

He couldn't help but think about how much he loved her and needed her in his life. "These past six weeks, pretending to be your fiancé, the man you are going to marry, have been the best weeks of my life. And tonight when I realized it was about to end, I had to face a number of truths. One of which was the fact that I have fallen in love with you."

Dana blinked, seeming thunderstruck. "You have?"

His smile showed a perfect set of white teeth. "Yes, and more than anything I want to make our engagement real." He lifted his hand to her face to caress her cheek.

"But getting what I want really depends on how you feel about me, Dana."

He saw the moment tears began forming in her eyes. "Oh, Jared, I love you, too, and more than anything I want our engagement to be real."

He chuckled with both joy and relief and pulled her into his lap. "I'm damn glad to hear that. So, Dana Rollins will you marry me? Be my wife, the mother of my children and the love of my life for always?"

He framed her face in his hands and continued. "Will you let that ring you're already wearing be a symbol of my love and promise? And will you believe that I will honor you, protect you and make you happy?"

He watched as more tears came into her eyes at the same time a soft chuckle escaped from her throat. "Yes, I'll marry you, Jared, and be all of those things."

An overpowering gush of happiness erupted from Jared's throat. "You do know this means you'll have all the Westmorelands as family?"

Tears made her choke back her laughter. "Thank God. I'd become attached to them and didn't want to give them up even though I thought this would be our last night together."

When his arms tightened around her she leaned down and rubbed her cheek against his chest. "You're a pro at making seductive proposals, Jared Westmoreland."

He grinned as his heart raced with unmeasured joy. "Am I?"

"Yes."

"Umm," he said as heat began stroking his body all over again. "I'm also pretty good at other things."

She met his dark penetrating gaze as she stared at him. "Are you?"

"Yes."

She leaned down, her lips mere inches from his. "Show me these other things. I dare you."

In one smooth move he quickly had her on her back. Their gazes locked and he knew he would love her for the rest of his life.

And that was the naked truth.

Epilogue

Two months later

Just as Sarah Westmoreland had predicted, there was another Westmoreland wedding before the end of the summer.

As Jared carried his wife down the church steps, she laid her head against his solid chest as rice rained down on them. Out of the corner of his eyes he saw his parents. He noticed his mother dab tears of joy from her eyes. To say she was happy was an understatement. But then, he knew she was already checking out her remaining five single sons to see who she should set her mark on next. He chuckled. She even had his cousin Chase within her intense scope. No one would be safe from matrimony if Sarah Westmoreland had her way.

When he and Dana were seated inside the limo, he

pulled her into his arms and kissed her with all the love he felt in his heart. His tongue swept inside to caress the walls of her mouth thinking that he would never get tired of the taste of her.

Their next stop was the grand ballroom of the Atlanta Civic Center. It amazed him how his mother and Aunt Evelyn, along with the long-distance assistance of his aunt Abby in Montana, were able to put together such an elegant wedding once he and Dana had set a date.

Jared released Dana's mouth and looked down into her smiling face. "How much ruckus do you think we'll cause if I tell the driver that we want to skip the wedding reception and go straight to the airport to catch our plane for St. Maarten?"

A smile touched the corners of Dana's mouth. "Oh, I think more than we're prepared to deal with. Your mother and aunts might never forgive us."

Jared grinned. "You're right. I guess the least we can do is show up."

"I agree."

He reached out and pulled her into his lap. It wasn't an easy thing to do considering her wedding dress. It was beautiful and she had looked gorgeous in it when she had walked down the aisle to him. Her best friend's husband, Ben, had given her away and Cybil had been her matron of honor. Delaney, Shelly, Tara, Madison, Casey and some of Dana's girlfriends from college had been her bridesmaids. Jayla had had to sit this one out since she was about to deliver at any moment. Dare had been Jared's best man and his brothers and the rest of his cousins stood in as his groomsmen.

Sylvester Brewster had asked to sing a song at the

wedding as a way to show his thanks for all Jared had done in getting him and his wife back together. After Jared had set up the meeting between them, the two had agreed to marriage counseling to make their marriage work. They were in love and wanted to put this episode behind them and move on.

Dana lifted her hand to admire her rings. She then looked at Jared's hand to see his matching gold band. She glanced up at him. She loved him totally and completely. An idea suddenly popped into her head. "Later tonight, when we're all alone I think we should play another game."

Jared lifted his forehead. "I thought Truth or Dare would be our final one."

She shook her head, grinning. "Why stop when you're having fun? And I have the perfect game for us."

She had peaked his curiosity. "And what game is that?"

"Spin the Bottle."

Jared smiled as he thought of all the possibilities and decided he could definitely put an interesting twist on that game. "Okay, I'm up for it."

Dana chuckled. "I thought that you would be."

And then with a shuddering sigh she pulled his face down to hers, her lips parting as she let him take possession of her mouth in a kiss that was full of all the passion she had come to expect from him. And as she returned his kiss with provocative urgency and overpowering passion, she knew that the best day of her life had been when she had agreed to become Jared's counterfeit fiancée.

* * * * *

Silhouette®

Desire®

presents the next book in

Maureen Child's

miniseries

*The Reilly triplets bet they could go
ninety days without sex. Hmm.*

WHATEVER
REILLY WANTS...

(Silhouette Desire #1658)
Available June 2005

All Connor Reilly had to do to win his no-sex-
for-ninety days bet was spend time with the
one woman who wouldn't tempt him. Yet
Emma Jacobsen had other plans, plans that
involved a *very* short skirt and a change
in attitude. Emma's transformation had
Connor forgetting about his wager—but
was what they had strong enough to last
more than ninety days?

Available at your favorite retail outlet.

If you enjoyed what you just read,
then we've got an offer you can't resist!

Take 2 bestselling
love stories FREE!

Plus get a FREE surprise gift!

Clip this page and mail it to Silhouette Reader Service™

IN U.S.A.
3010 Walden Ave.
P.O. Box 1867
Buffalo, N.Y. 14240-1867

IN CANADA
P.O. Box 609
Fort Erie, Ontario
L2A 5X3

YES! Please send me 2 free Silhouette Desire® novels and my free surprise gift. After receiving them, if I don't wish to receive anymore, I can return the shipping statement marked cancel. If I don't cancel, I will receive 6 brand-new novels every month, before they're available in stores! In the U.S.A., bill me at the bargain price of $3.80 plus 25¢ shipping and handling per book and applicable sales tax, if any*. In Canada, bill me at the bargain price of $4.47 plus 25¢ shipping and handling per book and applicable taxes**. That's the complete price and a savings of at least 10% off the cover prices—what a great deal! I understand that accepting the 2 free books and gift places me under no obligation ever to buy any books. I can always return a shipment and cancel at any time. Even if I never buy another book from Silhouette, the 2 free books and gift are mine to keep forever.

225 SDN DZ9F
326 SDN DZ9G

Name	(PLEASE PRINT)	
Address	Apt.#	
City	State/Prov.	Zip/Postal Code

Not valid to current Silhouette Desire® subscribers.

Want to try two free books from another series?
Call 1-800-873-8635 or visit www.morefreebooks.com.

* Terms and prices subject to change without notice. Sales tax applicable in N.Y.
** Canadian residents will be charged applicable provincial taxes and GST.
  All orders subject to approval. Offer limited to one per household.
  ® are registered trademarks owned and used by the trademark owner and or its licensee.

DES04R   ©2004 Harlequin Enterprises Limited

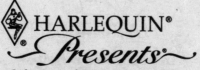

COMING NEXT MONTH

#1657 ESTATE AFFAIR—Sara Orwig
Dynasties: The Ashtons
Eli Ashton couldn't resist one night of passion with Lara Hunter, the
maid at Ashton Estates. Horrified that she had fallen into bed with such
a powerful man, Lara fled the scene, leaving Eli wanting more. Could he
convince Lara that their estate affair was the stuff fairy tales were made of?

#1658 WHATEVER REILLY WANTS…—Maureen Child
Three-Way Wager
All Connor Reilly had to do to win his no-sex-for-ninety-days bet
was spend time with the one woman who wouldn't tempt him. Yet
Emma Jacobsen had other plans, plans that involved a *very* short skirt
and a change in attitude. Emma's transformation had Connor forgetting
about his wager—but was what they had strong enough to last longer
than ninety days?

#1659 SECRETS OF PATERNITY—Susan Crosby
Behind Closed Doors
Caryn Brenley and P.I. James Paladin had a son without ever meeting face-
to-face *or* skin-to-skin. When Caryn learned James was her child's sperm
donor, she reluctantly agreed to let father and son meet. James jumped
at the opportunity, but pretty soon he wanted to get close to Caryn—the
natural way.

#1660 SCANDALOUS PASSION—Emilie Rose
Phoebe Drew feared intimate photos of her and her first love, Carter Jones,
would jeopardize her grandfather's political career. So she went to Carter
for help in finding them. But digging up the past also uncovered long-
hidden passion, leaving Phoebe to wonder if falling for Carter again would
prove to be her most scandalous decision.

#1661 THE SULTAN'S BED—Laura Wright
Sultan Zayad Al-Nayhal came to California to find his sister, but instead
ended up spending time with her roommate, Mariah Kennedy. Mariah
trusted no man—especially tall, dark and gorgeous ones. True, Zayad
possessed all of those qualities, but he was ready to plead a personal case
that even this savvy lawyer couldn't resist.

#1662 BLAME IT ON THE BLACKOUT—Heidi Betts
When a blackout brought their elevator to a screeching halt, personal
assistant Lucy Grainger and her sinfully handsome boss, Peter Reynolds,
gave in to unbridled passion. When the lights kicked back in, so did denial
of their mutual attraction. Yet Peter found that his dreams of corporate
success were suddenly being fogged by dreams of Lucy.…

SDCNM0505